Celebrating 100 years of romance with the very best of Mills & Boon

First published in Great Britain 2008
by Harlequin Mills & Boon Limited,
Eton House, 18-24 Paradise Road, Richmond, Surrey TW9 1SR

ISBN: 978 0 263 86618 6

77-0408

Harlequin Mills & Boon policy is to use papers that are natural, renewable and recyclable products and made from wood grown in sustainable forests. The logging and manufacturing processes conform to the legal environmental regulations of the country of origin.

Printed and bound in Spain
by Litografia Rosés S.A., Barcelona

Assignment: Seduction

by

Cathy Williams

MILLS & BOON
Pure reading pleasure

Cathy Williams is originally from Trinidad but has lived in England for a number of years. She currently has a house in Warwickshire which she shares with her husband Richard, her three daughters Charlotte, Olivia and Emma and their pet cat, Salem. She adores writing romantic fiction and would love one of her girls to become a writer, although at the moment she is happy enough if they do their homework and agree not to bicker with one another.

CHAPTER ONE

IT WAS nine-thirty at night. This was dark, unfamiliar territory and even inside the taxi it was freezing cold. Outside, with the wind rustling wrappers and paper along the street, the detritus of people who couldn't be bothered to find the nearest bin in which they could deposit their rubbish, it would be an icebox. A menacing, littered icebox. All that was needed now were a couple of howling, rabid dogs and some dustballs to complete the happy scene.

This had better be good.

'You sure you got the address right, lady?' The taxi-driver's eyes met hers in the rear-view mirror. 'Somebody meeting you at the other end? 'Cos this ain't the most savoury part of London.'

'Oh, somebody's meeting me all right,' Melissa muttered grimly under her breath. She crossed her slender legs and stared with mounting exasperation out of the window.

Even for him, this was too much. To give her forty minutes' notice, to *drag* her from the cosy warmth of her little flat not to mention the tantalising prospect of a ready-made meal curled up in front of the television, on the pretext that he *needed* to have a meeting with her *urgently,* didn't bear thinking about.

In the three years that she had been working for him, Robert Downe's utter disregard for convention had seen her working until three in the morning, taking notes at meetings conducted in the most unlikely places, being whisked off on his private jet an hour after she had stepped foot through the office door, but when she was home, her time had always been her own.

He demanded total commitment from everyone who worked for him, and from her he expected not only that, but a ready, obliging and preferably thrilled smile on her face to accompany his occasionally outrageous demands. But, as he had airily informed her at her interview, fair was fair. The minute she left the office, she would be absolutely free to shed her working clothes and indulge in whatever took her fancy, without fear that he would invade her privacy with unwanted work requests.

What he had omitted to mention was quite how thoroughly her well-paid, invigorating job would eat into so many hours of the day that the notion of having any sort of coherent, stable, routine private life was almost out of the question.

Her brilliant, temperamental, utterly dedicated boss didn't possess a nine-to-five mind and he was frankly bewildered by anyone who didn't share his lack of respect for clocks, watches and anything else that attempted to impose restrictions on the working day.

'Here we go, lady. Big Al's. Been in there a couple of times myself.' There was wistful nostalgia in the cab driver's voice as he harked back to what was undoubtedly his bad old days, judging from the unappealing sight that greeted her eyes. 'Looks worse on the outside than it is on the inside. And don't mind them blokes on the bikes. Gentle as lambs, they are.'

The herd of gentle lambs, some ten of them, began revving their motorbikes. One of them spat forcefully into the gutter, said something in a loud voice and there was a wave of raucous laughter.

I'll kill him, she thought to herself, *even if it means saying goodbye to the best job I'm ever likely to have. How could he have brought me here?*

'Want me to wait for you, just in case your mate ain't inside?'

'No.' Melissa sighed and handed over the fare, including a generous tip just in case she needed him sooner than she thought.

'Like hanging out with the rough sort, do you?' The taxi-driver caught her eye in the mirror and winked knowingly, a seedy gesture to which Melissa could find no response that came anywhere near the realms of politeness. Instead of answering, she opened the car door and swung her body outside.

The freezing cold attacked her like a vengeful lover that has been kept waiting for too long, and she pulled her coat tightly around her, shoving her hands into the pockets and walking quickly towards the bar, head down to protect herself from the biting wind. Outside the bar, a couple of loiterers were arguing over something. Out of the corner of her eye, she saw them pause in mid-flow to look at her and although her face registered no fear whatsoever, a thread of clammy apprehension uncurled inside her in sickening waves.

She pushed open the door and was greeted by a blast of wailing country music, a fog of smoke and the deafening babble of voices. In the middle of the room, a circular bar held sway, and around it was draped a collection of abnormally hairy men, largely dressed in faded denim. Sprinkled in between these flowers of shy beauty was a selection of blondes, mostly drinking out of bottles. Melissa had to steel herself against making an involuntary moue of distaste.

Towards the far end of the room, which was much bigger inside than it appeared on the outside, were three pool tables. In the background, Tammy Wynette continued to lament the passing of love.

It took a matter of seconds to locate the object of her irritation and she strode towards him, head held high, heels clicking purposefully on the wooden floor, hands still thrust into the pockets of her coat, tan-and-navy bag firmly secured under her arm.

A number of curious eyes followed her path across the room until she stopped, glaring, in front of her boss, legend in financial circles, talented, eccentric creator of vast wealth from little more than a background selling fish at Billingsgate Market with his father at the age of twelve, breaker of women's hearts, many of which she personally had had to deal with when love's first passion had grown bored and restless.

He was holding court at the far end of the room. He had pushed his chair away from the table, the better to accommodate his long legs and appeared to have his audience enraptured with whatever he was saying.

Somewhere very deep inside her, she could feel the full force of his overwhelming personality and his devilish good looks register on her consciousness. As it always did. In all the time she had worked for Robert Downe, he still had the power to unsettle her simply by the way he looked.

He was shockingly, no *scandalously,* good-looking. His hair was black and very short and his eyes were deep midnight blue, the blue of the sky when daylight has all but left and darkness is beginning to spread its wings. Sexy eyes. She might be immune to him but she had always reluctantly conceded the appeal he had over the female sex. Whatever their marital status, whatever their age, height, weight, class, profession or personality, his mere presence had always been enough to turn heads.

'You're late,' were his opening words, while three pairs of eyes settled on the petite, olive-skinned brunette with interest. Melissa ignored them all and focused her slanting brown eyes on her boss.

'Would you mind telling me *what* was so important that you had to *drag* me out of my warm flat, halfway across London at this time of the night? An urgent meeting, I recall you saying?' She tilted her small head meaningfully, and her thick, straight brown hair which she had left untied in her haste to meet her boss, swung against one shoulder. 'Strange, but the music is so loud here that I can't see how we could *possibly* have a conversation, never mind *conduct a business meeting.*'

It was one of her boss's occasional grumbles that no one, *but no one,* spoke to him as irreverently as she did, but it was, she knew from experience, the only way to deal with some of his more flamboyant moods. She worked too closely with him to be daunted by his forcefulness and anyway, it would have been out of character for her to tiptoe around him. In her own self-contained way, she was every bit as forceful as her boss.

'Whoa!' There were cries of delight all round and Robert flashed her a pained expression which she knew meant nothing at all. Had he forgotten that she had seen him in action over the years and knew that he was as humble and vulnerable as a barracuda on the prowl?

'See what I have to put up with?' he addressed no one in particular, and Melissa folded her arms and looked at him, gimlet-eyed.

'Yeah. Well, it beats Allie at the office,' one of the bearded men commented morosely. 'Sixty if a day and a shrew with it. Surprised I ever get any work done.'

'You don't work, mate. You draw.'

'You're an artist?' Melissa asked, side-tracked.

'Architect. For my sins.'

'With a face like that,' Robert said gravely, 'he had to go in for a job that kept him away from the public eye.'

Melissa felt a wicked urge to smile and had to remind herself that there was nothing to smile about because she had been rudely yanked from her privacy for what was fast appearing to be no reason at all. That was the problem with Robert Downe. He could move from infuriating to funny in the space of seconds with no recovery period in between.

'At least yours truly here doesn't have to rely on pretty-boy looks to get places,' he replied, grinning at Robert and winking at Melissa.

'Oh, my loyal secretary doesn't find me in the slightest bit good-looking, do you, Mellie?' He gave her one of those scorching stares from under his lashes. It was a look she had seen him direct at his leggy beauties from time to time, and she raised one eyebrow cynically.

'Which,' she said to her small audience, 'is why I'm still working for him.'

'You wouldn't swap me for all the tea in China. You know that,' he said huskily and she clicked her tongue impatiently.

'Work?' she reminded him. 'The reason I'm here?'

'Oh, if you must. Don't you want to relax for a few minutes?' He flashed her a winning smile which she returned with a warning frown. 'It's Harry's birthday today,' he said, tilting his head in the direction of a bearded hulk at the bar, and drinking straight out of the bottle. 'The big forty. The daddy of the lot. We've got a bit of a surprise for him.' Robert leaned over confidentially.

Melissa felt a twinge of unease at his closeness. Without consciously realising it, the lines between them were important to her. She needed the sanctuary of her home life, the untouchability of her privacy to keep his forceful personality at bay. She could handle him in a work capacity, where she was sure of herself and of her role but here, in a darkened bar, surrounded by his cronies, in an environment that stripped them of the invisible labels that defined them both, she realised that she was exposed and vulnerable in a way she didn't care for.

'Birthday cake,' Robert confided. 'Of the surprise variety. You know, one of those large affairs that house an attractive semi-clad woman who's a dab hand at a song-and-dance routine.'

'Oh, so nothing very chauvinistic then,' she said tartly. 'Is that why I'm here, Robert?'

'No, no, no!' He waved his hand vaguely at her. 'You're

worse than a minder,' he muttered ungallantly under his breath, while his friends watched them, avidly curious. 'Face of an angel, heart of a born dictator.'

Melissa flushed. Only because you don't know me, she wanted to retort, but instead she drew in a deep, steadying breath.

'Okay, we'll use Al's office. Half an hour and you can be on your way, back home so that you can tuck yourself neatly into bed and settle down for the night.' He stood up, towering over her, six foot one of sheer, unbridled masculinity.

Wealth had given him access to whatever he wanted. He could afford to liberally adorn his house with the most expensive paintings and rugs and he frequently indulged a taste for opera which seemed so out of keeping in someone who had probably never been to the theatre until he was a man, let alone an opera. But however much money and power he wielded, neither could subdue that hard restless edge which could be as intimidating to adversaries as it could be sexually arousing to women.

He had fought every inch of his way up and it showed in the aggressive, uncompromising angles of his face. He looked like a man who was afraid of nothing. In fact, the opposite—a man who was accustomed to instilling fear whenever it suited his purposes.

Happily, Melissa was thoroughly unimpressed by this particular quality. She looked up at him, one eyebrow expressively raised as he manoeuvred his way around the table and the clutter of chairs.

'When's the wedding, Robbo?' one of his friends asked and there was a round of bawdy laughter.

Melissa watched as dark color surged into her boss's face and for a few seconds, she witnessed one of those rare occasions when he appeared to be rendered temporarily speechless. It didn't last long.

'Ah, I wouldn't want to end up like you lot for all the

money in the world. Henpecked, the lot of you!' He grinned cheerfully at them.

'That's only because you haven't found the right woman to henpeck you into blissful submission. Yet. Although, the little lady next to you does show…'

'Right. Think I'll leave you bunch on that high note. Back out in an hour.' He reached down to the bottle on the table and then straightened with it loosely in his hand.

From a couple of feet away, Melissa watched him with peculiar intensity. Over the years, she had seen a fair amount of him outside work, but never totally relaxed as he was here. She had seen him in his capacity as her boss, entertaining clients, had even accidentally met him at the theatre once in the company of one of his glamour women. Always, he had been immaculately and expensively dressed in one of his many hand-tailored suits, only that primitive sensuality giving away his unpolished background.

Here, he was in faded jeans and a checked shirt which hung over the waistband and was rolled to the elbows, exposing his sinewy forearms. She looked away, idiotically ruffled by his blatant masculinity.

Al's office turned out to be a smart little affair, at odds with the rough-and-ready atmosphere outside. There was a small wooden desk, on which a computer terminal lay at rest and on another thin desk which protruded at right angles from this, were a fax machine, two telephones and several files, neatly stacked. The carpet was thick and cream and the walls were painted an unusual shade of green that gave the room a pleasant, leafy atmosphere. Robert took the chair behind the desk and gestured for Melissa to take a seat on one of the two facing him.

She had already removed her coat and draped it over the back of the spare chair. Now, she waited in silence, hands folded on her lap, legs crossed, for her boss to fill her in on whatever he had summoned her to say.

At least the slightly wild look had vanished from his face. At this moment in time, an unpredictable boss was something she could do without. In some of her more introspective moments, it occurred to her that there was something sad about her inability to cope with any shows of excessive behaviour. Hysterics, drunkenness, passion, intensity, they all fell into the same uncomfortable category, one that she was not equipped to handle. Restraint had been her mother's guiding principle and while a part of Melissa resented the limitations that placed on her behaviour, she was incapable of changing it.

'So,' he drawled, leaning back into the chair, which obligingly tilted back, affording him ample room to stretch his denim-covered legs onto the side of the desk. He linked his fingers together behind his head and proceeded to stare at her. 'What do you think of my schoolyard friends?'

Melissa looked steadily at him. 'They seemed very likeable.'

'My perfect model of restraint,' he said lazily, his eyes half closed as he continued to survey her. 'Do you ever shed your secretarial garb?' he enquired.

Melissa stared blankly at the wall behind him. This amused, frankly insolent line of enquiry was something she thought he had left behind a long time ago. When she had first started working for him, he had been intrigued by her personality. Intrigued that someone who was only twenty-two could be so self-contained, so cool, so collected.

He had seen nothing amiss in probing into her private life, asking questions about her likes and dislikes, her past, her background, even her sex life. It hadn't taken her long to inform him that her personal life had nothing to do with him, after which he had ceased peppering his polite see-you-in-the-morning chitchat with seemingly innocuous but bitingly curious questions about what she would be getting up to later on.

'Okay, okay!' He raised both his hands in a mock gesture

of defeat. 'I forgot. Remarks like that are strictly off limits! I can tell from that frozen look on your face!' But he was grinning, unperturbed by the fact that her face had remained rigidly unyielding. 'Work,' he carried on. 'I would have saved this for tomorrow, but as you know I'm off to New York in the morning and won't be back for a week, and this can't keep.'

'You could have telephoned me with your instructions,' Melissa pointed out.

'True. But it would have spoilt the surprise.'

A little thread of alarm shot down her spine. She didn't like his use of the word *surprise* nor did she like the expression on his face when he said it. He looked *quietly satisfied.*

'What surprise?' she volunteered tentatively. Surprises were something else she didn't much care for. How much her mother had to answer for! Without a husband, Melissa had always known that life couldn't have been easy for her mother, not least because the past had made her bitter and suspicious of other people and their motives.

Having watched her marriage finally crack under the weight of her second husband's rampant womanising, she had seen it as her divine mission to instil in her daughter a healthy disrespect for anything roughly resembling impulsive behaviour. Impulse, she was fond of saying, had been the downfall of your stepfather. Impulse, she would preach, shaking her head and pursing her lips into a thin line, had been the devil in disguise.

In fact, recklessness, in Melissa's mind, had come to rank as a grievous sin, punishable by something vague, unformed but definitely awful. By the time adulthood had arrived and with it an ability to put things into perspective, her mother had died and was beyond the reach of questions, and her daily homilies had turned into ingrained truths, stronger than reason and more frustratingly powerful than logic.

'There's a little job in the offing,' he said, watching her. 'Have you got a current passport?'

'You know I have,' Melissa answered, at a loss to know why she had to be called halfway across London to be told this.

'A good friend who can look after your flat for a while? You know, feed the goldfish, water the plants, et cetera.'

'I don't have any goldfish.' She gave him a perplexed frown. 'Just like I don't have a clue where this is leading. I'm sure the plants can survive for a couple of days anyway.'

Ominously, he sat forward and rested his chin on the tips of his joined fingers. 'The time scale is a little broader than that,' he informed her. 'A couple of months rather than a couple of days. And guess what, here's the really big surprise, *you're going home. Back home to Trinidad. A chance to relive all those great childhood memories.*' He sat back with an expression of triumph on his face. 'Now how's that for a surprise!'

CHAPTER TWO

MELISSA had ten days in which to arrange the technicalities of putting her life in England on hold for two months, and in which to contemplate the essential difference between *surprise* and *shock.*

Surprise, she could have pointed out, is when you open the door to your flat, thinking that the world has forgotten your birthday, only to be welcomed by all your friends and the sound of popping champagne corks.

Shock, on the other hand, is when your boss tells you that a gem of an idea which he's been nurturing from seed for months, little expecting it to ever really go ahead, has taken root, that his little gem of an idea involves an island you barely remember and rather wouldn't in any case and that you'll be going there with him on business.

'You never mentioned this to me,' was all Melissa could find to say after he had made his announcement.

'Excuse me while I reach for my hankie so that you can mop up your tears of delight at my little bombshell.'

Bombshell, she had thought, was the operative word, even though she had kept a steady smile on her face while she tried to formulate a few reasons why she couldn't possibly go with him.

Trinidad, sun-soaked, slow-moving, lush paradise,

belonged to her past. When she thought of it, she could barely conjure up memories of all those years she had spent there between the ages of five and eleven, when her stepfather had been posted on the island with the oil company for which he had worked. All she could remember were the rows between her parents. Long, bitter arguments that seemed to rage from one day into the other, with small breaks in between. As she had got older, the reason for the rows had become clear and with understanding came a new, deeper reason to run and hide from the shouting and the angry accusations and counter accusations.

She always felt that her aversion to confrontations stemmed from those childhood experiences when the raised voices of her mother and her stepfather had been enough to reduce her to a curled ball taking refuge in the corner of a room somewhere.

Of course, those memories were a secret, private place she shared with no one, least of all her boss.

'I couldn't possibly leave the country for months on end,' she had objected.

'It's eight weeks, not *months on end.*'

'What would happen to my flat?' She had only been a few seconds into her objections and she could see that already his temper was beginning to fray at the edges. 'I wouldn't feel happy about leaving it unoccupied for months.'

'Why not?'

'Because it might be broken into.'

'It might be broken into even when you're in it.'

'My plants…'

'Can be watered by a friend. You *have* got a couple of those lurking around, haven't you?'

'Of course, but…'

'No buts, Mel.' He had sat back in the chair and regarded her with fatalistic calm. 'Truth is, I never expected to get hold of this land, but I have and I'm going to need you there with me. You know the way I work and you can handle all the faxes and communications from London and New York without me having to hold your hand and explain things. You're single, unattached...' His voice had drifted speculatively into silence. 'Aren't you? No boyfriends hovering somewhere in the background, clamouring for tea at seven-thirty and sex every other night?' There had been a thread of insulting amusement in his voice when he said that.

'Why not *every night?*' she had snapped, instantly regretting her outburst when she saw the glitter of interested curiosity that lit up the deep blue eyes at her unexpected response to his needling. 'You can't leave the office for months, anyway.'

'I can do precisely as I like. I *own* the whole damn show or had you forgotten?'

And so every twist and turn she had tried had resulted in a dead end and she had found herself grudgingly and resentfully agreeing to his request.

Ten days to buy as much light clothing as she could find in shops that were fully stocked with coats, jackets and woolly jumpers, to arrange with her neighbour for her plants to be watered and the flat to be checked every so often, to sort out the distribution of work between the two girls who reported to her who seemed panic-stricken at the prospect of working on their own, until she reminded them that she would be calling twice a day to make sure that there were no problems.

The arrangements, she thought now, staring absent-mindedly through the airplane window to a bank of grey nothing outside, had been remarkably smooth. Robert had been right. She could shed her life for weeks on end without any difficulty whatsoever. There was no one who would miss her, no children to consider, parents to consult, lover to soothe. Not even a cat to fret over.

It gave her ample time to worry about the whole traumatic

exercise of returning to her past. It also provided a wonderful springboard for a new and equally disturbing line of thought which involved being in the presence of Robert Downe twenty-four hours a day without the respite of her private time away. True, the hotel would afford her a certain amount of protection but the thought of eating lunch and dinner with him made her feel a little ill.

He hadn't given her a schedule of his work timetable while out there, but she quickly decided that whatever it was, she would subtly alter it to ensure that business meetings with his lawyers and contractors and designers and architects and all the other people who would be turning his land into a hotel, took place over lunch and dinner. During which time she would either be present, taking notes whenever necessary but basically sliding happily into the background, or else in her hotel room, away from him completely.

By the time the plane landed at a little after six-thirty in the evening at Piarco airport, nerves had been joined by a healthy curiosity about the place she and her mother had left behind fourteen years previously, stripped of all their possessions, fleeing like a couple of thieves in the night while her stepfather remained on the island with the latest in his line of outside women.

There was growing familiarity as she made her way through passport control, lining up behind all the other non-Nationals. She collected her luggage and made her way through customs, to find a sea of people crowding the barriers outside.

The heat was thick and furnace-like. The navy-blue slacks and blouse she had worn for the journey adhered themselves to her body like cling film while she anxiously cast her eyes around for her lift to the hotel.

Robert Downe was nowhere to be seen.

A short, black man asked her if she wanted a taxi and she abstractedly refused, still holding out some hope that her wretched boss would appear even though she knew him well enough to realise that if he had become involved in a phone call five minutes before he was due to leave for her, it was more than possible that he wouldn't show up for a good while yet. She had dragged her cases to the side and resignedly sat down for an indefinite wait on one of the benches, when a skinny, middle-aged man with coffee-brown skin approached and asked her if she was Melissa James.

'Yes!'

'Mr. Downe sent me for you. The car's over there.'

'How did you know who I was?'

'He said that if I arrived late, I would find you waiting somewhere at the side with a long-suffering look on your face, Miss James.'

Remind me, she thought sourly, to murder my boss as soon as I see him and scatter his body parts to the four corners.

'And where…is…Mr. Downe?'

'Back at the Kiskidee. He was hard at work when I left.'

They had reached a dusty saloon car parked at an angle in the No Parking zone. He slung her cases in the trunk, opened the back door for her, and as soon as he had settled into the driver's seat, they sauntered slowly off. It was a relief that the driver was uninterested in making conversation. It gave her time to settle back and watch with a mixture of nostalgia and unease as the landmarks of her past unfolded before her eyes.

Lots seemed to have changed, yet nothing much. The roads were better, at least so far, and as they entered Port of Spain, she could see all the old familiar buildings still there, rubbing shoulders with a few new office blocks. Dim memories of childhood friends stirred at the back of her mind and she wondered what they were up to now. All ties had been severed when they had returned to England and now she could only vaguely recall names and faces.

The drive, stopping and starting and finally moving

smoothly as the city was cleared, then the outskirts, then the mountainous winding road along the rocky, lush northern coastline, took over an hour and a half. By the time they hit the first beach along the route, one she remembered very clearly, it was too dark to see anything and she was too tired to be disappointed.

She just wanted to get to the hotel now, have a shower and put her feet up in the privacy of her room.

She must have nodded off because when the car shuddered to a stop, her eyes flew open to see the indistinct outline of her boss peering through the window at her.

'Here in one piece!' he said, pulling open the door so that she nearly fell out of the car and had to regain her balance. 'Sorry I didn't make it to the airport to collect you myself.' He held her by her shoulders at arm's length and stared down at her. 'I've missed you! There's a pile of work waiting inside.'

'Thanks,' Melissa answered drily, shrugging out of his grasp. 'Nice to feel wanted.'

She fell into step alongside him, while ahead of them, their driver carried her suitcases as though they weighed nothing. All around them the noises of the night, crickets and frogs and the rustle of small animals in the undergrowth, were like a background symphony. She could hear the night breeze sift through the trees and bushes and the sound of the ocean like steady, even breathing, rising and falling and forming a soothing lullaby with the other sounds of the night.

'Where's the hotel?' she asked, perspiring profusely as they made their way along a narrow path bordered with foliage and flowers. They had stopped outside a house and before answering he pushed the door, which had been slightly ajar and turned to her.

'House, actually.'

She stepped through the door into a tiled, airy room, and rounded on him, aghast.

'What do you mean *house*?'

'Just dump the bags by the table, Raymond. I'll take them to her room in a little while. See you tomorrow. Tell your wife there's no need for her to show up before nine.'

'You told me we'd be staying in a hotel!' Melissa said shrilly, as soon as they were alone.

'How does it feel to be back home?'

'Now you inform me that we're sharing a house?'

'You look as though you could do with a shower. You're perspiring. It's those clothes you're wearing.'

'This is a ridiculous situation! I can't stay in a house with you for the next two months!'

'Why not?'

'Because *I just can't*.'

'Even if I promise not to touch you? However tempted I might be by your sizzling sex appeal and that wicked little way you have of looking at me out of the corner of those big, brown eyes?' He grinned and she glared at him. 'Okay! I reserved two rooms at the nearest hotel but even the nearest was too far away from the land, so in the end I had to rent this house. It's more convenient. Now why don't you go and freshen up and then join me outside on the porch. I'll fill you in on what the general schedule's going to be over the next week or so.'

'Robert…' She sighed and folded her arms. The thoughts in her head were too big to explain rationally and her most disturbing thought was the one that was the least possible to elaborate. How could she tell him that she could cope with all his moods, keep up with the frenetic pace he set himself, remain as cool as a cucumber when he stormed through the office because something was bugging him, but the thought of being in his company when work no longer comprised the four walls around them, sent her into a state of mild panic? How could she ever explain that his deliberate teasing threw her into a tizzy, even though she didn't know why?

'Yes?'

'Where's my bedroom?'

'Along the corridor to the right. Last on the end. See you in a minute.'

He was whistling as he walked away.

This had not kicked off to a good start. This had all the promise of being one of her bigger life mistakes. No safe hotel with lots of people around, no sanitised conference rooms booked for work and meetings. Just the two of them and without the trappings of an office, who knew what mischief he might feel inclined to indulge in. His warm, sexual teasing could be as intrusive as fingers along her body and although she had always made sure to keep the lines between them very clear, she hadn't cared for a couple of his insinuations earlier on. She would have to be as business-like as possible, even if she risked seeming a bore in the process.

She showered quickly and hurried outside, where the night air felt cool against her and the sound of the sea was steady and rhythmic, like an African drumbeat. From the open patio, she could look down the small slope and glimpse beach through the coconut trees and bush that fringed the little inlet.

'I'm on the beach!' His voice floated up to her mingled with the sound of the surf and when she squinted into the darkness, she could make out a shape standing ankle-deep in the water. 'Stairs down to the left!'

Melissa licked her dry lips and tentatively made her way down the concrete steps to the beach, holding on to the iron railings on the side with one hand, clutching her notepad and pen with the other.

The dark shape on the beach was waiting patiently for her, looking at her slow progress down, his arms folded, his feet planted solidly on the sand, slightly spread apart. It was too dark to see the expression on his face, but his silhouette was reminiscent of something powerful and indestructible.

'I thought we were going to do some work,' she said, when she finally hit sand. The inlet was small, with a thick fringe of bush and trees spreading densely back from the sand, climbing up the small incline that led to the house. The sand felt firm and compacted under her feet and the sea was a black swell beating against the sand.

'I changed my mind,' he freely admitted, walking towards her, then past her to what she now saw was a towel spread on the sand, and upon which he flung himself, linking his hands beneath his head and staring up at the starless sky. 'Actually, I thought you could tell me a bit about the country. After all, you lived here for…how long…? Five years? Six?'

'I don't remember much about it,' Melissa said warily, watching his prone shape on the sand, the way his short, baggy T-shirt rode up to expose the firm skin of his torso, the length of his muscular legs. 'We left when I was eleven.'

'Why was that? Daddy got a transfer back to England?'

'No,' she said flatly. 'What are your plans for tomorrow? Will I be staying put here and working or do you need me to come with you to meetings?'

'Sit down. My neck's beginning to hurt looking up at you. Besides, I can't see your face when you're standing so far away. It's too dark.' He shifted a bit and patted a little free patch of towel next to his hip. 'It's very disconcerting addressing a faceless disapproving voice. Come and sit by me and tell me all about what you *do* remember of the place. Come on,' he said persuasively, 'I don't bite, you know.' He laughed throatily. 'So you can relax. Look at where we are, for heaven's sake! Warm night air, sea, sand, stars in the sky…no place for frosty disapproval!'

'I'm here to work, Robert,' Melissa reminded him. 'If you wanted someone to enjoy a romantic, tropical setting with you, then you should have considered bringing your…your…' Her voice, firmly assured when she had started her little speech, petered out into awkward silence.

'My...my...*lover?* Was that the word you were searching for, Melissa? Haven't got one at the moment, actually. Besides, the last thing I need out here is a lover. I just need *you* to relax a bit. This isn't an office now. We're both going to have to adjust to that fact.'

'We only came as far as this beach a few times,' she said eventually, yielding to his request for information simply because she knew that if she didn't, he would pester her until he got what he wanted. She made no move to sit next to him, though. That was taking relaxation a little too far for her liking. A sudden, graphic image of her thigh bumping against his made her brain temporarily cease functioning, then it recommenced, sending messages to her mouth that it should continue speaking, whatever the content.

'Most people tend to stop at Maracas Bay which is further back. This is just a little too far for a day trip. I...it's a lot more developed than I remember. Are there any shops around here? There weren't fourteen years ago. Just vegetable and fruit stalls by the side of the road. Any shopping entailed a trip to the city.'

In between her babbling, her mind toyed with the delicious and illicit image of his body brushing against hers, the feel of his hard, muscular flesh pressing against her, the touch of his fingers along her stomach and thighs and breasts. She gulped and felt faint. Rather than perch on his towel and send her already fevered mind into further overdrive, she slid down onto the sand and pulled her knees up to her chin, hugging them with her arms.

'No shops,' he confirmed, sitting up and looking at her. 'You'll get your shorts dirty sitting on the sand. In case I haven't mentioned it Raymond's wife will be coming in daily to clean and cook, and yes, you'll have to come to some of my meetings with me to take notes but a lot of the time you'll spend here. I've managed to get hold of everything you'll need to work. Fax machine, computer, printer, stationery, the usual.

'Tomorrow we'll be going to the city centre. I have a meeting with the lawyer and in case you're worried that I'm going to take advantage of your presence here to turn you into a workhorse, you're wrong. You'll work the same hours you work in England and you can do what you like with your free time. Did you keep in touch with any friends over here…?'

'No.'

'Why not? Or is that question off limits as well?' He had a knack of making her reticence sound like a sinister cover-up.

'*As well?* As well as *what?*'

'Really want me to tell you?' he asked softly. 'Put it this way, Mel. You've worked for me now for over three years. You probably know me a damn sight better than any of my women ever have, yet I don't know a thing about you. I haven't got a clue what makes you tick.'

'That doesn't make any difference to how I do my job.' Her heart was thumping. In the darkness his face was all shadows and angles and impending threat.

'I never said it did. I do find it a bit odd, though. What have you got to hide?'

'Nothing. I'm reticent by nature.' She stood up and brushed herself down with trembling hands. The silence between them took on a sound of its own, as definite as the sound of the sea or the fluttering of a bird's wings inside a cage.

'So tomorrow…' she said, clearing her throat.

'Meetings. I'll want you with me. After that…we'll see how things progress…no point planning too far ahead…is there? Life tends to short-change people who are stupid enough to do that…'

CHAPTER THREE

MORNING came earlier than Melissa expected. There was no alarm clock to drag her out of bed at seven-thirty, but nevertheless she was wide awake by quarter to six. The curtains at the windows were light, airy voile and were not designed to prolong sleep, whatever the constitution of the bedroom's occupant. Not a room for nursing a hangover.

She luxuriated in the king-size bed for a few minutes, drowsily taking in her surroundings which she hadn't really paid much attention to the night before. The wooden flooring, with a few bright rugs strewn here and there, the light wicker furniture, the pale walls with indifferent seascape scenes set in wooden frames adorned with sea shells.

It was tempting to fling on some shorts and a T-shirt and amble down to enjoy the scenery, but that posed the small problem of bumping into her boss, who might be similarly prowling around at this ungodly hour. She had spent an unreasonable amount of time lying in bed the previous night, trying to work out what it was about Robert that had unnerved her from the minute she stepped foot in the house the evening before. When she tried to analyse what he had said, her memory failed her and really, he had acted no differently than he always did, treating her with the outspoken, occasionally exasperating openness that came from familiarity.

So why had she suddenly found his presence so disturbing? She had scurried back to the house from the beach, grateful for the cover of darkness, like a scared rabbit that has only just managed to escape a predator.

It wasn't as though she didn't know him and wasn't all too familiar with his moods.

She took her time getting dressed, and then gazed at her reflection in the mirror. Her face was smooth and olive-hued, her features pleasant but unremarkable, her hair shiny and well kept but certainly no exotic mane of blonde curls. She lacked the voluptuous curves of the sort of women her boss was wont to court. It was ridiculous to imagine that he would see her in a different light simply because the normal constraints of work had superficially been removed, and vice versa. Clothes, she reminded herself, do not make the man.

By six-fifteen she was warily tip-toeing her way out of her bedroom, ears pricked for the first hint of noise coming from his, and hearing nothing, she scampered out of the house with a sigh of relief and headed down towards the beach.

In the greyish, early morning light she could appreciate what the blackness of the night before had successfully concealed. The lush foliage interspersed with leaning coconut trees, pressing against the sides of the railings, desperate to break the slender iron barriers and clamber over the concrete steps.

As she skirted down the twisting concrete steps, she caught different glimpses of the sea. The beach itself was small, a tiny cove which, she recalled, became virtually sandless when the tide was high. Now, the tide was low and the sand was scattered with the dregs that had been washed up from the ocean overnight. Twigs, seaweed, bits of wood, shells, broken chunks of coral.

As soon as her feet touched the beach, she removed her sandals and felt the sand between her toes, not white and grainy but pale brown and compacted.

'I didn't expect you up so early.' The booming voice came from somewhere to the left of her, out of sight but too close for comfort, and she momentarily froze.

He emerged from behind a bank of bushy undergrowth clad only in swimming trunks with a towel slung over his shoulders. His short hair was still slightly damp, which made it stand up in spikes. His body was powerful and sinewy and shamefully brown. How was this situation ever going to work out? Secretaries shouldn't have to confront their bosses when said bosses were virtually naked. Pin-striped suits protected both parties from that sort of ridiculous familiarity.

'You didn't wear your swimsuit,' he accused, eyeing her tidy shorts and polo shirt outfit up and down. 'This is the best time for a swim, you know,' he continued conversationally, either unaware of her embarrassment or else choosing to ignore it. 'Cool, peaceful.' He massaged his neck with the towel and then gazed upwards at the sky with what she thought was an undue amount of dramatic appreciation. 'The perfect time to be at one with Nature.'

'I had no idea you were so spiritual,' Melissa said, snapping out of her nervous reverie. She walked briskly away from him, towards the sea and then stood at the edge of the water, her sandals still in one hand, aware that he had followed and was standing a little behind her.

'Didn't I say that there were lots of things you didn't know about me?'

'No. You said that I knew everything about *you* and you knew nothing about *me*.'

'So you *do* listen to what I say, even when it has nothing to do with work,' he breathed against the nape of her neck. 'Sometimes I wonder. You look as though I'm speaking a foreign language whenever I make a personal remark.'

'Do I?' Melissa asked innocently, not daring to move an

inch because she would probably bump into him and the thought of that brought her out in a cold sweat.

'You know you do. But heck, you're a shy private person…you might not believe this, but I'm a very shy private person as well…'

That made her swing round with a laugh of sheer disbelief. 'Oh, please!'

'I am,' he protested meekly.

'Since when?' She looked at him with frank amazement, unconsciously registering the fact that he hadn't yet shaved and the dark shadows around his chin lent him the rakish air of a pirate.

'What makes you think that I'm not?' he countered neatly, folding his arms and looking down at her with interest.

'The fact that you shamelessly intimidate people when you want to? And don't try to deny that, I've sat in enough meetings with you to know the methods you employ and the adjective shy doesn't spring to mind here. And what about your women? How many of them have trooped into your office over the years? Distraught and wailing because you've decided that their expiry date has arrived? You don't seem to mind that most people know all about your private life!'

'They only think they do,' he replied smugly. 'When I want, I can be as secret as the grave.'

Melissa gave him a wry look of scepticism and tilted her head to one side, 'Well, that's as may be.' She kicked her feet in the sand.

'Sure, the odd blonde has occasionally put in an appearance in my office…but that just means that I don't mind a bit of speculation on the part of my loyal staff when it comes to that…it'd be quite a different matter if I were serious about a woman. There's no way I wouldn't respect her privacy.'

'Uh-huh?' she grinned, turned her face to the rising sun and closed her eyes, loving the smell of the salty air and the feel of the breeze blowing warmly against her face.

'You'd be very surprised,' he said gruffly. 'Look, why don't you come in for a swim? There's no need for us to start work yet.'

'A swim?' Melissa's eyes snapped open.

'Why not?'

'Because...well because...'

'You *did* come equipped with a few swimsuits, didn't you?'

'Yes, of course, but...'

'But what? I'm not asking you to perform a striptease! Can't you take off your working hat just for a minute and loosen up? I'm not going to bite you!'

'I never said that you were!' Her face reddened at the accuracy of his shot. 'A short swim *would* be nice, as a matter of fact.'

Fifteen minutes later, she was back on the beach, this time wearing a black bikini with a big T-shirt over it. She had brought one of the beach towels with her and she rested it neatly on the sand, along with the divested T-shirt, and peered out towards the horizon. The sun was edging up quickly and bringing with it the promise of fierce heat.

She tentatively strolled down to the edge until the water was lapping against her ankles. When she looked up, she could see his head far out in the distance, past the breakers.

'Coming?' he shouted, 'it's all perfectly safe! I've vetted it personally for sharks!'

In which case, she thought cynically, what are *you* still doing in the water?

She took a deep breath as the cold water slapped against her body, then she dived under a wave and began swimming out. She was fairly out of breath by the time she reached Robert, who was waiting for her on his back, arms behind his head.

'You have to admit that this is refreshing,' he told her, staring up at the sky while she looked at his averted profile and paddled inelegantly in the undulating water. 'Lie on your back. Like me. Or you'll get out of breath.'

'What time is the meeting?'

'Eleven. Just imagine what England would be like now… cold, wet, grey… I think I could retire to a place like this.' He paused for a fraction of a second. 'Did you miss it when you left?'

Melissa flipped onto her back and considered his question, or at least considered whether or not to answer it.

'Not for long. Things were hectic when we came back. I was busy with a new school, new house, new life…'

She sighed involuntarily and he said, without hesitation, 'Why do you say *new life?* Surely it was just a change of environment? Everything else was the same?'

'Not quite.' She closed her eyes and allowed herself to relax and enjoy the effortless bobbing of her body on the surface of the sea. 'Stop probing,' she added for good measure, and smiled when he chuckled next to her.

'Now why would I do that?' he asked equably. 'We're not in England now. You can't threaten to walk out…' He was referring to the threat she had made a long time ago when his curiosity had gone a little too far. 'You're my prey here,' he murmured in an amused, husky drawl. 'Nowhere to run…just you, me…the opportunities to get to know one another better are limitless…' He laughed throatily, then loudly as she spluttered down into the water in alarm.

'Sorry,' he said, when she surfaced for air, her face red with confusion at his words. 'I didn't mean that. It's always so tempting to get behind that prim and proper air you carry about with you like a suit of armour.' He was looking at her, his eyes squinting against the sun. 'You should be careful, you know,' he murmured, warming to his subject, as her skin went a couple of shades deeper and her brown eyes interlocked with his blue ones, 'some men are turned on by that look of Victorian modesty. Knocks the socks off the usual tarty blondes who leave nothing to the imagination…'

'What are you trying to say?' she whispered foolishly, and he grinned at her. 'Oh, shut up,' she sputtered indignantly, looking away. 'I'm going inside. I'm getting a little waterlogged here.' She ducked under the water and began swimming back to shore. She heard a smooth sound alongside her and glanced across to find him cutting an easy path through the water at her side, overtaking her. She deliberately slowed down to give him time to get well clear of her and then she watched covertly as he left the calmer waters of the deep behind and effortlessly dived beneath the bigger breakers near the shoreline, rising up beyond them until he was standing, calf-deep and watching her.

Distracted, she felt herself ambushed by an enormous wave that seemed to come from nowhere, and as she tried to push herself under, it lifted her off her feet. Fifteen seconds in a washing machine and then she was spat out, dazed and standing inches away from him. She glared up and thought that if his grin got any wider he would have to have his face surgically stitched back together.

'Quite a tumble,' he said gravely, mouth still twitching as he looked down. 'And bits of you are showing the after-effect.'

Melissa followed the direction of his eyes. In the underwater chaos, part of her bikini top had ceased to do its job and one breast was half out with more than a glimmer of brown nipple exposed. She gave a shriek of horror and adjusted her swimsuit but she could feel the colour rush into her face.

She couldn't look at him. She just couldn't meet those wickedly amused dark blue eyes. She remained where she was in frozen silence for what seemed like decades, although she knew that it could only have been for a few short seconds.

If she had had more experience with men, she might have found the right words to laugh the whole thing off, but she hadn't.

'No need to feel embarrassed, Mel,' he pointed out. 'I've seen women's bodies before.'

'That's not the point. You've never seen…you've never seen…'

'*Your* body before?'

'This is a ridiculous conversation!' Her face was bright red and she had never felt further from the serenely efficient secretary who could survive her boss at his most demanding without turning a hair. She had always thought that she knew how to handle him, but she was fast discovering that her skills in that area were in urgent need of polishing. Those snippets of charm and wit which were second nature to him were diluted when in England. Now, without anyone else around, she could feel them bombarding her and her reaction was one of confusion rather than indifference.

'You're absolutely right,' he agreed amicably, and she silently released a sigh of relief that he had decided to drop the conversation. 'I may have seen lots of women naked, but I've never seen *you*. Not that I haven't done my fair share of wild imagining.' He laughed as she fell into his trap, mouth half open with a retort, and she gritted her teeth together and made a stifled, frustrated sound under her breath.

'*You*, if you don't mind me saying, are the most…the most…'

'I know,' he answered placidly, 'that's why you love me.' He grinned at her and nodded in the direction of the house. 'Shall we go up for breakfast? Before you burst a couple of blood vessels?' He stepped aside with a gallant bow, allowing her to precede him, which put her in the unnerving position of knowing that his eyes were firmly focused on her as she manoeuvred the steps back up to the house.

She decided that she would very rapidly have to re-establish the status quo between them. Things were slipping and he was getting under her skin in a way he never had before, or perhaps had never had the opportunity to before. Ringing telephones, people bursting into the office unannounced, meetings and trips abroad, they all tended to reduce conversations to the pertinent, and when she accompanied him in her capacity as secretary to his thousand-and-one business engagements, it had always been simplicity itself to make sure that dangerous atmospheres of intimacy were not established.

She could kick herself for not being a bit more thorough in her line of questioning about this particular trip. She had happily assumed a number of things, most importantly that they would be staying in a hotel rather than in a house miles away from civilisation.

As soon as she reached the top of the steps, she paused to allow him time to fall in beside her and remove his vantage point of five paces behind.

'I'll just have a shower before we eat and get down to work,' she told him briskly.

'I'll make sure that the files are ready and waiting,' he told her, with equal briskness. 'And you'll be pleased to hear that Raymond's wife, Denise, will be in the house. Cook, cleaner and unwitting chaperone.'

'I don't need a chaperone,' Melissa answered smartly, not looking at him, 'I'm here as your secretary and that's as far as it goes.' Just in case he started getting any ideas, she thought. The Devil works on idle hands and hands that are housebound can get very idle indeed, especially when they're accustomed to being kept busy. It was as good a time as any to establish one or two boundaries before she found herself with a situation for which she was not prepared.

'Of course,' he said a little too quickly.

'Good.' They had reached the house and through the open patio doors, she could make out the shape of a dark-skinned rotund woman, who was sweeping the tiled floor with single-minded zeal.

'Besides,' he whispered wickedly into her ear at about the same time as Denise looked up at their approaching figures with a smile of recognition, 'I'd hate to shock poor Denise. Wouldn't you?' At which he drew away and entered the house with a carefree, merry whistle on his lips.

CHAPTER FOUR

MELISSA thought that the drive to Port of Spain would be an hour and a half of acute, badly concealed embarrassment sitting in close quarters with a man whose presence was growing on her like a burr under her skin, but in fact the drive sped past.

They both sat in the back seat with Robert's Louis Vuitton briefcase open between them, and together they went through the daunting stack of files concerning the property, using the particular shorthand which they had developed unconsciously over time.

Her eyes barely left the papers in front of her, her questions were succinct, as were his replies and by the time they had cleared the winding, rugged coastline with its confusing baggage of ill-formed memories, she had managed to absorb all the relevant facts about the purchase.

'I still don't understand why you chose this particular island,' she said, allowing her eyes to drift thoughtfully over the scale drawings of the hotel in front of her. 'Tourism isn't big over here. In fact, most people haven't heard of the place.'

She crossed her legs, primly clad in her knee-length flowered skirt and absent-mindedly pushed a loose strand of hair away from her face. She had tied her hair back and as usual, her technique was already letting her down.

'I know. Clever, wouldn't you agree?' he said with satisfaction, stretching his arm along the back of the car seat so that his hand was disturbingly close to the back of her head.

Melissa wondered whether she would have been as hypersensitive to that one week ago. How many times had they shared a taxi? Hundreds, she was sure. Or quite a few at any rate. He *must* have sat exactly as he was sitting now, with his arm extended behind her, his legs crossed so that his knee wasn't a million miles away from her own. Why was she now finding it difficult to concentrate on anything except the tantalising possibility that he might accidentally brush the back of her neck with his fingers?

'Would I?' she asked, conscious that she was leaning forward by a couple of crucial inches in an attempt to avoid the possibility of her head crashing into his hand.

As if reading her mind, he removed his arm, but only to shift the briefcase off the seat onto the floor, so that he could adjust himself into a more comfortable position, then back went the arm and forwards went her head.

'Think about it, Mel, the usual Caribbean haunts are becoming saturated. It won't be long before they're overstocked with hotels and the discerning tourist begins to cast his curious eyes around for somewhere a little less developed.'

'At which point, those curious eyes fall on this underdeveloped island and lo and behold, what should be waiting but your hotel?'

'Very good!' he said approvingly, settling a bit more comfortably in the seat and spreading his long legs wide to accommodate the lack of appropriate space in the back of the car. His khaki-clad knee inevitably rubbed against her leg and now, with her body straining away from his leg and his hand, she could uncomfortably feel her muscles begin to ache. She sighed and relaxed, determined to ignore his proximity.

'I got the land at a very good price and I've done my

homework on the place, checked out all the attractions. It's just going to be a question of targeting the right market.'

The car bumped over a giant-sized pothole in the road and she found herself crashing inelegantly into the man next to her.

'The roads don't seem to have improved from when I was last here,' she muttered, shuffling away from him. 'I don't think your flood of potential tourists are going to warm to the bumpy roads.'

'Nonsense. They'll find it charming. Don't you know *anything* about human nature?'

Melissa turned to him, eyebrows raised. Robert, she had realised over the years, rarely professed ignorance on any subject, including those on which he was totally ignorant. She had known him to deliver lectures to some of the most important financial gurus in the city, having prepared nothing on the subject and with only cursory preparation of the details he needed. He would simply charm his way through an hour of speech, relying on his wit and his ability to think on his feet, to get him through. And get through he invariably did. He was the sort of man who would stick in the throat of the conventionally educated academic.

His education had been erratic and conducted as much in school as in the street, his university had been the proverbial university of life but his brain was unsurpassable. She doubted that there were many subjects he would not have been able to grasp in the minimum amount of time and tales of his exploits in the world of finance were legendary throughout the company. Everyone knew how he had risen from street trader to a man whose reputation for financial wizardry was beyond compare. He seemed to have been born with an innate ability to judge the movement of the money markets and by the age of twenty-seven he had already made a fortune.

All the more fascinating to his legion of admirers, was the fact that he seemed to have remained unchanged by his position. He dressed without respect for convention, paid no lip service to politeness unless it was deserved and had almost no tolerance for idlers.

Human nature, though, was quite a big subject for Robert to declare himself an expert on.

'Don't tell me you've been keeping a degree on psychology hidden up your sleeve,' she said, turning to look at him. She wished she had brought her sunglasses with her instead of leaving them on her dressing table, because the sun pouring out of the bright blue sky was blinding. Robert, naturally, had had a bit more foresight, and he slipped on his dark Oakley shades so that his eyes were conveniently obliterated while she had to content herself with shading hers with one hand.

'You *know* I'm little more than an uneducated lout,' he said grinning. 'I never came close to a university to get a degree on *anything,* never mind psychology! No, I just understand what makes people *tick,* if you know what I mean. People don't go abroad so that they can experience exactly what they left behind at home. Think about it, if *you* went abroad somewhere, would you want everything to be the same as in England? Same roads, same food, same shopping, same scenery? You might as well just stay put!'

'Some people like the creature comforts,' she pointed out stubbornly. 'They might find bumpy roads a little annoying, and then have you considered the fact that this hotel is going to be miles away from civilisation? No shops, no night-life, no clubs, no chemist, a couple of restaurants but nothing fancy?'

'Of course I've considered it!'

'And…?'

'Another plus, of course. *You* might call it boring, but others would find the solitude and isolation quite an attraction.'

'*I* wouldn't call it boring at all, actually,' Melissa couldn't resist pointing out at the last minute. 'I happen to *enjoy* peace and tranquillity.'

'So you wouldn't be bothered by the lack of night-life?'

'No.'

'Or entertainment?'

'No.'

'And what about those missing shops and chemists?'

'I was trying to point out potential drawbacks,' Melissa told him patiently.

'I know,' he replied humbly, 'and I'm grateful to you for doing that. I have no idea where I'd be if it weren't for you, bringing me down to earth whenever my wild schemes threaten to get out of hand.'

Melissa looked at him narrowly to ascertain if he was poking fun at her, but it was impossible to tell because of the sunglasses which, offputtingly, reflected her face back at her.

'So if *you* wouldn't find any of those things drawbacks, why shouldn't there be other people who think like you do?'

'Would *you* enjoy being so far out of the mainstream traffic?' she said, throwing the question back at him. 'I wish you'd remove those shades,' she said irritably.

'Sure.' He slid the shades down his nose so that he was peering at her over the top of them and with a click of her tongue, she reached out and removed them altogether.

'*You,*' he said lazily, 'can be a very masterful woman when you want. I like that.'

'You haven't answered my question.' His tendency to digress away from the serious business of work to the dangerous matter of her personal life, was threatening to get out of hand. At first, she had thought that it might have been her imagination, but she was beginning to clue in to his technique, which seemed to be based on lulling her into a sensible conversation, only to hijack it somewhere along the line.

Scarily, she was beginning to discover that his unsubtle intrusions might be unwelcome, uninvited and downright aggravating, but they were also fiercely thrilling.

'So I haven't,' he agreed, resting his head back against the seat and closing his eyes in the manner of someone giving something a great deal of thought. 'Let me put it this way,' he said eventually. 'I may not be able to spend the rest of my days cut adrift from the human race, or at least cut adrift from all the mod cons that make up day-to-day living, but I would happily spend a couple of weeks in total isolation. Just the roar of the sea, the shrieking of the gulls, the sound of the breeze blowing through coconut trees at night. What better than a walk on the beach under a sky as black and soft as velvet?'

What better indeed?

Melissa's eyes became unfocused and she gazed dreamily past Robert's shoulder.

'With the sea lapping against your ankles?'

Melissa nodded in appreciation.

'And the sand indenting under your feet? Hand in hand with your loved one…have you ever done that?'

'God, no.' She laughed as she swam out of her pleasant reverie about black skies and lapping water and holding hands with loved ones. 'Maybe I'll consider it, though, when the loved one appears on the horizon.'

'And then,' he continued crisply, 'aside from the benefits of solitude, there's the wildlife. Did you know that one of the most important bird sanctuaries is only a short drive away?'

'Yes. I did, as a matter of fact,' she answered, surprised as yet another memory dislodged itself from its burial place. Under the force of her mother's bitterness and her vivid memories of leaving under a black cloud of unhappiness and parental despair, she had totally forgotten that not all of her past deserved to be wiped out. There *had* been good moments and the bird sanctuary in question had been one of them. She had gone with her class on a school trip and she could remember the excitement, at the age of nine, of the long drive to Asa Wright, the thrill of seeing all those birds, a profusion of colours, the tour through the reserve, the bathing in the small, freezing waterfall, the denseness of the rainforest around them.

She turned to Robert, her eyes alive, and for no other reason than the sudden need to share her memory with the man next to her, she told him about the trip, the fun she had had. She could even remember some of the weird names of the birds. Honey-creepers, white-bearded manakins, and of course the hummingbirds.

That memory seemed to open a door to other, less painful memories, and she found herself telling him all about other places she had visited as a child. He was a good listener. Attentive, asking just the right questions, and they arrived in Port of Spain, the capital, without her even realising that their long drive was at an end.

'Sorry to have been so boring,' she apologised with a grimace, as Raymond opened the back door for her and waited for her to get out. The heat was blistering after the air-conditioned coolness of the car.

'You were anything but,' he said seriously, turning to give Raymond a few instructions, then looking down at her. 'You keep your past so well hidden, that I always assumed that there *was* something to hide.' He took her elbow and ushered her through the small garden that led to a black-and-white Colonial-style house, with its intricate woodwork and veranda that skirted the circumference of the dwelling.

'It's not quite as straightforward as that,' Melissa told him, with a shadow in her eyes. For once, she had no inclination to retreat from confidences. She had nothing shameful to hide but she had been *made* to feel as though she had by her mother, who had never recovered from her husband's infidelity and had dragged her daughter down with her.

'We'll pick this conversation up later,' he promised, but her eyes were shuttered and she stared straight ahead as they climbed the six steps up to the front door of the renovated house. Next to the door was a discreet brass plaque with the name of the lawyers on it.

'There's nothing *to* pick up,' Melissa said truthfully. 'Most people have untidy childhoods and I'm no exception.'

He pressed the doorbell then leaned against the wall and stared down at her.

'On the contrary. I find you quite exceptional. Are you aware that you...'

What he had planned to say was lost as the door was opened by a neatly dressed girl with a broad smile. They were shown through an open-planned office, where the sound of hands flicking quickly over computer keyboards was nicely accompanied by the intermittent ringing of the telephones.

Chris Ali's office was off the main area and after the initial rounds of introductions, during which he expressed polite interest in the time she had spent in Trinidad, they settled down to business.

After all this time, Melissa still admired the way her boss could control the ebb and flow of meetings with effortless ease. Every point put forward by the lawyer was probed, laid bare and only put to rest if Robert was completely satisfied with the conclusion.

They meticulously went through page upon page of detail, ranging from the location of the land to the land boundaries, to intricate tax questions which she faithfully transcribed but barely understood.

Coffee was brought in, and after an hour, some sandwiches on a plate and glasses of freshly pressed, ice-cold orange juice.

Watching how Robert operated was an object lesson in brilliance. His body language was perfectly relaxed, utterly at ease, but his eyes were watchful and his questions were polite but cleverly leading. He plied the young lawyer for opinions on the economic market, the trends in tourism, the financial climate, long-range forecasts for the American dollar, and Melissa could see his brain ticking away as he compiled the information and processed it all for further use.

Hotels were something of a pet hobby for him. With the advent of his first million had come the birth of his fascination for hotels, mostly in weird and wonderful places catering for an adventurous minority, travellers as opposed to tourists.

He expanded on the various styles of architecture of his various hotels and how dependent it all was on the culture, not to mention the weather, of the country. He picked his lawyer's brain mercilessly about advantages and disadvantages of the style of hotel he had chosen, nodding when an idea was mulled over, taken on board and stored as a possibility.

Melissa couldn't transcribe expressions, but she knew him well enough to absorb when something of particular importance was being said so that she could incorporate it in the private report she would write up for him.

Sometimes he would quiz her afterwards on what sort of *feeling* she had had about someone or something that had been said. Meetings with him were not places to relax, and by the end of their session, she felt suitably drained and eager to get back to the house.

'I could fall asleep,' she yawned, as the car picked up a pace and Port of Spain was gradually left behind.

'Don't tell me you've got jet lag.'

Melissa didn't answer. She closed her eyes and let her body slump in the car seat, not caring whether she was jostled into him or not. He obligingly settled comfortably into the back seat as well. One unfortunate jolt and they would collide like two rag dolls.

'I hope not,' he continued, turning his head to look at her from under his thick, black lashes. Melissa reluctantly opened her eyes to find his face rather closer to hers than she expected. 'Because we have one more stop to make before we get back to the house.'

She stifled an inward groan and tried to perk up at the prospect of another gruelling meeting. Her wrist was still killing her from the last one!

'What's that?'

'The land. The all important piece of land that's going to enable me to build the most stupendously unique hotel this island has ever seen. It's a five-minute drive past the house and I thought you'd be interested in having a look.'

'Oh, yes. Great.'

'You're already beginning to go brown, do you know that?' he murmured, and she straightened herself and shook off the remnants of exhaustion.

'I tan quickly,' she said, adjusting her skirt and her legs at the same time.

'Your skin is like satin.' He stretched out one finger, trailed it softly against her cheek and by the time her body had reacted with a start, the offending finger had been removed and his hands were decorously linked on his lap.

'What was that for?' she demanded in a shaky voice.

'Nothing. I just wanted to see if it felt as soft as it looked.'

'Well, don't.'

'And it does.'

She didn't answer. Instead, she stared straight out of the window at the trees and houses that comprised the scenery. Where his finger had touched, burnt as though electric volts had been put through her skin and in the enclosed space of the car, she could feel his eyes on her, doing as much damage as his single finger had done, turning her blood to glue and her pulses to mush.

'Did you manage to get everything Chris said?' he asked, changing the subject with such ease that she realised, with a mixture of relief and disappointment, that he was unaware of the effect he had on her. She nodded with her head still averted and only relaxed when he began chatting about work and plans for the hotel. By the time they bypassed their house and reached the plot of land, it was still hot but the sun was beginning to turn the deep, mellow colour that precedes nightfall.

'If you remember the plans,' he said, once they were standing outside the car and gazing at the land from various angles, 'the front will be on the very edge of the drop and the rooms will be stepped so that every balcony overlooks the sea. The pool will be over there.'

Melissa did her best to obligingly follow the direction of his finger, but he had unbuttoned his shirt and her eyes, with a stubborn will of their own, kept slipping to that slither of bronzed torso peeking out from between the open shirt. His body was hard and muscled and toned to perfection.

While he enthused on the subject of eight huge rooms, four above four, positions of bathrooms and laundry rooms and kitchens,the intricacies of the health and safety regulation laws that required exits at appropriate distances, she fought a losing battle not to stare as a light breeze whipped his shirt further apart and exposed yet more tantalising skin.

His waist and hips were narrow enough for his khaki trousers to dip sexily down as he walked. The gap between waistband and skin was just big enough for a finger to be inserted.

She closed her eyes, perspiring slightly, stepped backwards and hurtled into an uneven patch of rocky ground.

CHAPTER FIVE

THE pain in her ankle was the equivalent to a mosquito bite in comparison to the pain in the curve of her back, where she had unluckily crashed into mud and rock. The ground had clearly been brushed and probably flattened, as well, but it was still uneven enough to make the wearing of sensible shoes an absolute must. Melissa's shoes were sensible in the carpeted environment of an office but utterly useless in this sort of terrain. From her inelegant position sprawled on the ground, she could see that one of the offending articles of footwear was lying several inches away from her foot and the other was half off.

Why? Why, why, why? When she was trying so hard to claw back some of her well-controlled, efficient, unflappable secretarial sang-froid, did she have to trip and fall flat on her back because she had been too busy trying not to look at her boss's body? He had always *had* the same body and she had always been in full possession of twenty-twenty vision, so why was she suddenly so stupidly transfixed by the sight of his bronzed torso, however well muscled it was? Or had she *always* stared at him, but safely, from behind her well-tailored suits and well-tailored, bland expressions? That was a thought she decided quickly not to pursue.

She tried to stand and weakly fell back to the ground with a moan of pain and self-disgust.

Robert was covering the distance between them and before he could say anything, she looked up at him, squinting against the fading sun, and blurted out, 'I'm all right.'

She propped the palms of her hands behind her and made a determined attempt to support her words with some action. Unfortunately, her body refused to cooperate.

He knelt down, instantly invading her body space.

'No, you're not.'

'Robert, please. I'm fine. Or at least, I will be in a minute.' He had shifted his attention from her face and was now contemplating her foot, then, to her intense discomfort, he gently touched her ankle, his hands soft and exploratory, sending little waves of startled awareness up and down her spine.

'It's not broken at any rate.'

'Oh, good!' Melissa answered in an unnaturally high-pitched voice.

'Now, I'm going to ask you to support yourself as much as you can.' He had swivelled back around and was peering at her from his disconcerting squatting position. She knew, without a shadow of a doubt, that this was the most embarrassing situation she had ever found herself in. Aside, she thought, from the beach scenario of the evening before.

One embarrassing situation could be termed an unfortunate mistake but what, she wondered, would one call two? Especially in the space of as many days? Was there any psychobabble jargon for someone's body deliberately ambushing their intellect?

'I have a bruise, Robert. I haven't cracked my spine in five places.'

'How do you know?'

'How would *you?* You're not a doctor!'

'Just do as I say, Mel.'

She grudgingly inched her body up slightly and rubbed the tender spot at the base of her spine.

'Right. I'm going to carry you back to the house.'

'Don't be ridiculous! You can't *carry me back to the house!* You'll collapse!'

As soon as the words left her mouth, she knew that she had waved a red flag to a bull. Now, if the house happened to be ten miles away and situated up a ninety-degree incline, he would rise to the challenge of getting her there, caveman style. She could read as much from his raised eyebrow and the glint of his teeth as he smiled wryly and indulgently at her. With a sigh of defeat, she let her body go limp as he lifted her off the ground in one sweep, swiftly and gently enough for her to feel no sharp twinges.

Although sharp twinges might have taken her mind off the hardness of his chest pressed against her like a branding iron and his masculine aroma that filled her nostrils like a mind-distorting drug.

'This really isn't necessary,' she muttered feebly, closing her eyes in a damage limitation gesture because *feeling* his body was enough to contend with, without having to see it, as well, in all its annoying glory.

'Yes, it is. Haven't you read your manual?'

'What manual?' She risked opening one eye to see that the house, thankfully, was now within range of sight.

'The updated Employee Manual, Code 256.'

'I've never heard of it.'

'In that case, let me summarise Section 12, Employer/Employee Responsibility, as defined by the government under the 1982 Act.'

'What are you talking about?' she asked, distracted enough to forget the aroma and the muscled torso.

'To paraphrase, "the employer," namely myself…'

'I'm aware of your status in the firm!' she snapped, sinking back into her state of mortification.

'"…is responsible for the safety and health of his employees and should any misadventure arise due to negligence on his part, then he is legally bound to compensate said employee for aforementioned.'"

Melissa wondered whether he could possibly be seen to hold himself responsible for her inability to drag her eyes away from his body. Perhaps if he had seen fit to be several stone overweight…

'I mean,' he added softly, looking down at her and addling her further, 'what if you decide to sue me? It's my duty to do my utmost to ensure that you receive prompt attention.'

It was getting quite dark now. She couldn't clearly make out his expression, but to her ears, what he was saying was beginning to sound a little ridiculous. Was he making fun of her? Was there really some manual that she had failed to read during her term of employment with him? She couldn't believe that there was. She had always been so assiduous when it came to details like that.

'Naturally, I shall call a doctor out as soon as we reach the house…although, I have to warn you, he might be a while. It's dark, we're far enough away from civilisation for us to be on another planet, and as I'm finding out very quickly, things and people don't tend to move at the speed of light over here.'

'There's no need for a doctor,' Melissa nearly begged. She had visions of her mortification being dragged out over a period of hours when in fact she knew that all she needed was to swallow a couple of painkillers, put her feet up and probably take it easy on the walking for a day or two.

'I know you're just saying that because you don't want to make a fuss, Mel. I haven't worked with you all these years for nothing.'

'I'm saying that because there's nothing wrong with me that a good night's sleep won't cure!'

'Sleep doesn't cure a sprained ankle,' he pointed out. They had finally made it to the house and he pushed open the kitchen door which had been left ajar for them. 'At least, not to my knowledge.'

'No, but two aspirin and some basic dressing should do the trick and I am more than capable of attending to both.' With that firm statement, she could almost *feel* her business-like efficiency creeping back into her bones. 'I did that first-aid course a couple of years ago, and I passed with flying colours.'

He had walked over to the sofa and he now gently deposited her on it, then vanished to have a word with Raymond, which was slightly deflating since she could feel herself gathering pace in her figurative secretarial garb and she would have appreciated making him aware of the fact.

When he returned, it was with a glass of water and two painkillers.

'Raymond is going to go back to the land to get your shoes. Here are some aspirin.' He handed her the water and she picked the tablets out of the palm of his hand, then he dragged the solid coffee table a few inches toward the sofa and perched on it.

'Now, your ankle and your back…'

'Yes,' Melissa said eagerly. 'painkillers for the back and I was telling you about my first-aid skills. If I tell you what to bring, then perhaps…'

'No can do.' He was shaking his head ruefully.

'What do you mean *no can do?*'

'If you don't want me to call a doctor, and I think we could get away without one, then it's my sole responsibility to tend to you. Need I refer you to the previously mentioned "Employer/Employee Act?"'

He bent down and a flare of unreasonable panic rushed through her as she felt his arms circle her prone body.

'*What* are you *doing?*'

'Taking you to your bedroom. I've turned your air-conditioning on so it's nice and cool in there.' He strode purposefully in the direction of her bedroom while she clamped her teeth together in frustrated impotence.

'There's no need for all this,' she virtually wept, as he laid her on her bed. 'Those painkillers are kicking in. All I need now is a good night's sleep and…'

'"Employer/Employee Act?"'

'Will you *stop going on about that!* I've never even *heard* of such a thing.'

'I knew there had to be something my incomparable secretary had missed! Now. The ankle's a little swollen but looks fine. I'll have a look at your back first. On your stomach.'

Could things get worse?

She eased herself over and felt alarm and dismay flood her body as he eased her shirt up to the level of her bra strap and gently pulled the skirt and knickers down together to the firm swell of her buttocks. 'Ahhh.' Fingers against flesh, light, feathery touches that made her shiver and did unfathomable things to her pulse rate. 'Superficial bruising. Not very pleasant to look at but no swelling, which is a relief.'

Such a relief that he nevertheless continued to skim his fingers along her back and make knowledgeable noises under his breath while she did her valiant best to control her accelerated heartbeat and appear composed. As though this was all in a day's work.

Eventually, he neatly pulled her shirt down and informed her that he would rub some cream on the bruise but a diet of painkillers might well be necessary over the next couple of days. She omitted to point out that he was merely echoing what she had said herself only minutes before.

'Now, ankle.' He disappeared for a while, allowing her some privacy to arrange herself on her back with her clothes respectably tucked around her prone body, and returned with a larger than average first-aid kit. 'You'll need a bath before

I can get to work on seeing to these cuts and bruises. I'll run one for you.'

Melissa eyed him balefully as he headed into the en suite bathroom and began running water, testing it occasionally until the temperature was right.

'Now don't move a muscle' he called, meeting her eyes in the large mirror above the double basins in the bathroom. 'I'll have to bathe you.'

It took a few seconds for that to sink in, then her mouth dropped open in unconcealed horror.

'Absolutely not!' His hands? On her naked body? His eyes scouring the curve of her small breasts, possibly even brushing against them? She didn't care how many naked women he had clapped eyes on in his lifetime, or touched intimately for that matter. There was no way under the sun that she would allow him to get near her even if that meant remaining in a state of mud-encrusted shabbiness until all her bruises had vanished.

'Employer duties?' He strolled out of the bathroom and each step was a threat that had her sliding back into the mattress as though hoping for an unexpected escape route through it.

'Can take a running leap!'

'But, Mel.' He shook his head in an unconvincing display of paternalistic concern. 'We've known each other for years! You can't possibly feel uncomfortable in my presence!'

He paused at the side of the bed to stare down at her and she glowered up at him from her disadvantaged position.

'Robert...' she said warningly, and he cocked his head to one side, listening mode.

'Do I understand from that tone of voice that you don't want me to bathe you?'

'Very perceptive.'

'But...' He frowned. If she weren't busily engaged in

trying to squash an uncharacteristic state of panic, she would have openly guffawed at his ludicrous changes of expression. Did he think for a minute that she was going to fall for that *Trust me, I know what's best* look? 'How are you going to get yourself to the bathroom, never mind manipulate yourself into the bath, soap, get out of the bath, towel yourself dry and get into some fresh clothes?'

'Which particular manoeuvre is posing a problem for you, Robert?'

'All of them.'

'In that case you'll just have to take my word for it that I can manage. Now, if you don't mind…' She looked meaningfully in the direction of the bedroom door while he continued to survey her with the expression of someone having difficulty in absorbing a certain train of thought.

But, thankfully, he left. And to ensure that his absence did not come to an untimely end in the middle of her laborious ablutions, she hobbled painfully to the door, locked it and then set about the time-consuming business of trying to get clean.

As he had shrewdly predicted, every move awakened new and hitherto undiscovered areas of pain. Having made it to the bathroom, she felt in need of several hours' rest. Exhausted, she sat on the lid of the toilet and contemplated the business of now removing all her dirty clothes, getting into the bath, and then repeating the whole thing backwards.

It took approximately forty-five minutes. She knew because she timed it on the clock propped up on the dressing table in the bathroom. Ten minutes to remove her clothes, a few torturous minutes climbing into the bath, a wonderfully long and enjoyable soak, which she could have remained blissfully lapping up if her ears hadn't picked up the distant but persistent sound of knocking on her bedroom door, accompanied by Robert's distinct though undefined voice. It didn't take the IQ of Einstein to figure out that he was probably yelling to find out whether she had drowned in the bath.

With a gleeful giggle, Melissa held her nose and submerged herself under water so that she couldn't hear a thing. When she reemerged, it was to find that his voice had miraculously disappeared.

By the time she had killed a few more minutes, taking her time in the bath, *just to prove to herself that she wasn't going to be intimidated into getting out before schedule,* then slowly dried and shoved on the easiest things she could grab hold of, her stomach was beginning to rumble with hunger.

'I know I look awful,' was the first thing she said to him when she finally left the comforting four walls of her bedroom and ventured out into the living area. He had showered and looked annoyingly refreshed and sinfully handsome in a pair of dark green shorts and an old cream jersey which did a great deal for his body and not much for her struggling self-composure.

'It was the least cumbersome thing I could manage.' She made her way to the chair, sat down and winced.

'Time for a few bandages? Cream for the back might have to wait until tomorrow. I'm afraid the first-aid kit wasn't quite as comprehensive as I expected. Remind me to put that on my list of *musts* for the hotel. Every possible nonprescription medication under the sun.'

'For the difficult guests?'

He walked over to her, knelt at her feet, which made her feel wickedly in control of him, and held her foot in his big hands, then he pulled out a long strip of bandage, like a magician pulling a rabbit out of a hat, and he began to wrap her ankle with professional speed.

'*Difficult*'s not quite the word,' he said drily, his hand moving quickly over her foot. 'Some might say that in the absence of a readily available doctor, something or someone must be available on site for anything that might happen. What do you think of hiring a medic full-time to stay in the hotel?'

He stood up, surveyed his handiwork with smug satisfaction although she could see that his mind was already running away with other thoughts. It was amazing how thoroughly you could get to know someone when you worked closely with them. She had never realised it before, but she knew far, far more about him than she would ever have imagined. It was only now, and here, confined as they were in an unnaturally close situation, that she became aware of how easily they communicated without going down the usual avenues of speech. She could read his moods, understand what he wanted to say almost before he verbalised it himself.

'Food?' he looked at her enquiringly, and she in turn looked at her neatly wrapped foot, and nodded absent-mindedly at him, head down-turned. When she next looked up it was to find him standing by the kitchen doorway, staring at her with a plate of sandwiches in his hand.

'Something light all right with you? Denise made some sandwiches. Wasn't sure when we'd be back, you know how meetings have a tendency to drag on.' He pushed himself away from the door frame towards her.

'I'm impressed,' Melissa said, as he sat down opposite her and deposited the plate on the table between them. 'I never knew you were that much of an expert in wrapping feet.'

Something else that was odd, and even more disconcerting was the fact that neither of them had noticed, certainly, *she* hadn't until now: the lines of demarcation, such as they were, between them, had vanished. Here he was, bringing food to her, when normally she would be attending to him, bringing the cups of coffee, ordering food to be brought to the office on the odd occasion when they had had to work late. Yet, worryingly, it felt natural and comfortable.

'That's because you've never been the damsel in distress.'

He stretched out his long legs, leaned forward to take one of the sandwiches and bit lustily into it. 'And I've been waiting long enough to show you my potential as a knight in shining armour.' He looked at her for such a long time that she could feel the colour slowly invade her face, like a fever. 'You don't believe me, do you?' he asked softly.

'Of course I don't.' Her voice was shaky, as was her laugh. 'You were asking my opinion about employing someone at the hotel full-time as a doctor,' she reminded him, looking away. Thank goodness he couldn't read minds. What murky things he would find in hers, she shuddered to think. Things she herself barely knew how to address. Disturbing things best left unspoken.

'So I was,' he said eventually, after a silence long enough to make her aware of the fact that he knew she was changing the subject and he was willing for the moment to oblige her diffidence. 'What do you think about that idea?'

CHAPTER SIX

'YOU can't come into Port of Spain with me,' Robert told Melissa the following morning when she had hobbled out of the bedroom and into the sun-drenched living room. There was a slight morning breeze blowing, bringing the smell of the sea with it, and an overhead fan made it blissfully cool.

'I've *got* to!' Melissa protested, sinking into the chair and feeling grateful yet ridiculously pampered as Denise fussed around her with a breakfast of warm coconut bake, butter, guava jelly and fresh fruit juice. 'I'm here as your secretary! I know my ankle's going to make things a bit slow, but if you can bear with me, I can more than manage to do my job!'

'Out of the question.'

'Why? *Why* is it *out of the question?*' Her voice was thick with dismay. She was being paid an astronomical bonus for this trip and the thought of having to abandon her duties because of her own stupidity was enough to bring a flush of guilty colour to her face.

'"Employer/Employee Act,"' he reminded her gently. He had finished eating his breakfast and now sat back to enjoy his coffee, shifting his long body until he found the most comfortable position. He was already dressed for going out—long cream-coloured trousers, subdued cream shirt with fine, navy lines running down it, brown loafers worn without socks so that she could glimpse brief flashes of brown ankle whenever he adjusted his legs.

She was staring. Again. She did it unconsciously. Frightening. Even more frightening was the notion that he might have noticed, that he might have spent the last three years *noticing* something she had never even been aware of herself before.

'Oh, not *that* again,' she groaned, and he shook his head ruefully.

'Afraid so,' he murmured, looking at her over the rim of his coffee cup with a *That's life, what can a poor man do?* expression on his face. 'As your employer, I can't do anything to compromise your health and dragging you around town from meeting to meeting from dawn till dusk isn't exactly going to do you and your bruised body parts a world of good.' He lifted his shoulders, helplessly.

'And don't I have a say in all of this?'

'Absolutely none. But don't worry, you'll have more than enough to deal with here at the house. The fax phone's been going every three seconds since I got here. Lord knows, you'd think my people couldn't manage a day without me.' He smiled smugly at her and this time it was her turn to look mildly amused at his arrogance.

'Hopeless, isn't it,' she agreed with a straight face, 'being needed so much. Mind it doesn't go to your head and give you an outsized ego. Sir.'

He grinned at her. 'Well at least your sense of humour's intact, even if it *is* at my expense.'

'I wasn't making fun of you,' Melissa informed him with wide-eyed innocence, looking down when he raised his eyebrows with outright incredulity at her statement.

''Course you were. I think you see it as one of your missions in life. To make sure that I keep my feet rooted firmly on the ground. My mother would have approved of you.' He stood up and stretched, then stuck his hands in his pockets and looked down at her. 'Now are you sure you can get from A to B without too much difficulty? I won't be gone long, just until after lunch.'

'I'll be fine. And I thought I couldn't possibly go with you because you were going to be trekking from meeting to meeting.'

'Slight exaggeration. I want you to make some enquiries into what we talked about yesterday.'

'On-site medic for the hotel?'

'Yup. There must be other hotels in the same situation as we are. Out in the middle of nowhere land. Maybe you could call a few and ask them how they handle the problem. There are maps of the island in the office so you should be able to pinpoint the relevant places. Anything else I need to tell you?' he asked absent-mindedly.

'Yes. Have you brought your electronic organiser over? I need to start filling in your diary.'

'Haven't actually.' He grinned winningly at her, like a little boy seeking approval before he confesses to some misdemeanour. 'I've been using scraps of paper.'

'Very naughty,' Melissa said, unable to resist grinning back at him because it was so *very like what he would do.* For someone who was known as a mover and shaker in the dangerous financial world of the city, he had a few stupidly endearing idiosyncrasies that would wrong foot the most cold-blooded of the opposite sex. He was the ultimate in power, wealthy and razor-sharp intelligence, a man who could and did, build castles in his head and then proceed to fearlessly transform them into reality, yet he still managed, at will, to project an elusive air of vulnerability. Naturally, he was capable of ruthlessly using those very traits to get what he wanted and from whom. She decided that she must, at all costs, remember that.

'I know. That's why I need you so badly to manage me.'

He glanced at his watch, then back at her. 'Right. I'm off now. Raymond's going to drive me to town but Denise'll be here until I get back. She's going to prepare some lunch for you so you don't have to worry about food, and I'll stock up on the way back. You just need to concentrate your pretty lil' head on your work and I'll be back before you know it.'

'Absolutely no need to rush.'

'What makes you think I don't want to?' he asked, tilting his head to one side.

A remark to which she responded by tilting *her* head to one side in a manner identical to him, and saying, sweetly, 'What makes you think I *want* you to?' Before he could see that as anything in the least flirtatious, she carried on, in the same breath, 'I shall work a lot quicker if I'm left to my own devices, unless, of course, you have things to dictate to me...?'

'One or two letters. I'll need you to set appointments for me to meet with the architect and the interior designer, as well as the tourism guy.'

'On individual scraps of paper?'

'I'll get a desk diary from somewhere and bring it back with me this afternoon, although,' he added en route to the door, 'I happen to find the scraps of paper a lot more individual...'

'...But a lot less practical!' she called after him, mentally plotting the day ahead, relieved that he wouldn't be around. She heard the bang of the front door and actually gave a sigh of sheer bliss at the sudden sense of peace.

She could hear Denise in the kitchen. She would pop her head in briefly to let the older woman know where she was, then she would devote the morning to working solidly. She had never been one of those people who could contemplate a day of complete inactivity with an easy mind. She was happiest when occupied and the sea breeze combined with the daytime noises of the birds and the rustle of the coconut trees and leafy foliage was enough to bring on a deep sense of contentment.

She tried to remember whether, as a child, these surroundings had ever had the same effect on her, but if they had, then the memory eluded her. She remembered the heat vividly enough, but contentment was something she had only fleetingly glimpsed in her life, usually, now that she thought about it, at the end of a long but satisfying day at work, when she and Robert had accomplished everything on the agenda and had celebrated in quiet camaraderie with a take-out meal at the office before pushing off to their respective houses.

Except, she thought now, Robert wouldn't have been *pushing off to his house,* would he? Replete after a take-away Indian or Chinese, happy at the prospect of curling up into bed, just managing to catch the last of the ten o'clock news? For him, the night would have been just beginning. He would have been pushing off, all right, but pushing off into the arms of some blonde bimbo somewhere for a light supper followed by something far more interesting than an empty double bed and a cup of decaffeinated coffee.

Her mouth tightened and she walked slowly, like a very old woman, towards the kitchen, where she informed Denise of her whereabouts.

'Just in case you think I've dropped off the side of the cliff,' she said, smiling.

'Mr Robert says that you know this place.' Denise flashed crooked, white teeth in her direction. 'He say you lived here when you was a chil'. That true?'

Melissa nodded. 'Only for a few years when I was very young. I barely remember it.'

'Must be nice coming back, eh?'

'Strange, if anything.'

The other woman resumed wiping the kitchen counters. 'Different coming back here with a nice young man, though, eh?'

'Well, he's nice enough and young enough, I guess, but he's certainly not mine.'

Denise stopped and gave her a beady look. 'He might be by the time you'se ready to leave.' She gave a cackle of laughter and shook her head, shaking with mirth.

No wonder her stepfather had found infidelity so easy under the hot, unforgiving sun, she thought, making her way to the improvised office. Sex was always available, always on offer, and the heat and the sun and the lazy atmosphere were all ingredients that went into the hot pot of adultery.

He couldn't keep his hands off the women, her mother had railed until the day she died, unforgiving to the bitter end. *Men! Never think about the wife they're two-timing.*

Was that why she, Melissa, had never gone out of her way to cultivate long-lasting relationships with men? Because deep down she was guided by still more pearls of wisdom gleaned from her mother? She had never thought about marriage as something particularly desirable and whenever she heard of someone who had become the victim of her partner's infidelity, she hardly ever registered surprise. After all, her stepfather had been very meek and mild to look at.

Her mind, released on this train of thought, continued to worry away at it throughout the morning, while the rest of her functioned happily on automatic, replying to all the faxes that had accumulated over the past twenty-four hours, making phone calls to England, sorting out problems long distance, and laboriously checking up with every known out-of-the-way hotel on the island to find out what they did about on-site medical services.

She had switched off the air conditioner in the room, preferring to open the windows and turn on the overhead fan, and the balmy breeze had her yawning every half an hour, even though she didn't feel in the least bit sleepy.

She was only aware of the passing of time when she heard the click of the office door and looked up, expecting to see Denise, only to clap eyes on Robert instead.

'What time is it?' she gasped in surprise, swivelling on her chair so that she was facing him instead of the computer terminal.

'A little after three.'

'A little after three!'

'I know, I know. Time flies when you're having fun, doesn't it?' He strolled across the room to her desk and perched on the edge, then he picked up a stack of typed letters and began flicking through them absent-mindedly.

'How did your meetings go?'

'Meeting. Just the one.' He pushed himself off the desk, went to the generously sized two-seater sofa and sprawled languorously on it, his long legs extending over the arm, his hands folded beneath his head as he yawned and stared lazily in her direction. The action of raising his hands to his head had yanked his shirt out from the waistband of his trousers so that bare skin peeped out at her. Her small, pointed breasts began to ache treacherously.

'And how did it go?' *Just the one meeting? Did one meeting going over fairly routine stuff with a surveyor take over four hours?* 'If you let me have the reports I can sift through them and get out any letters you want to send by tonight.' *Maybe he had decided to do a little island exploring on his own? And why not. There was a hell of a lot to see and there was no need for him to rush back to the house, not while she was competently holding the fort.*

'Sure. Everything was pretty straightforward, though. No unforeseen problems. I'll just need a letter confirming the meeting and the outcome. Report's on the dining room table.'

And of course, the chartered surveyor would have recommended somewhere lively for a spot of lunch and Robert Downe being Robert Downe, lively was an atmosphere he took to like a duck to water. Not a man made to sit for long on his ownsome when there would doubtless have been lots of pretty girls around, if only in the form of waitresses.

'How about you? Any problems?'

'Huh?' She dragged her wayward mind back to the matter at hand, namely her boss, indolently reclining on the sofa and staring at her with smoky-blue eyes.

'Work? Gone to plan? Found everything you needed? No hitches?'

'Good, yes. Fine. Letters typed. One or two issues back home. I've jotted down the problems for you and said that you'd send them an e-mail when you get back.'

He was undoing his belt, much to her consternation. He whipped it off and then tucked his hand a fraction under his waistband. Her aching breasts, exasperating enough to deal with, had now summoned various other zones of unwanted arousal, including between her thighs, which was growing damper by the minute.

She shifted uncomfortably in the swivel chair, aware of his eyes on her.

'I've also done a bit of checking around on the subject of the on-site medic,' Melissa carried on hastily. Small, cheese-cloth-flowered dresses and bare legs were no way to assert a sense of authority in front of one's boss.

'You're fidgeting. You shouldn't sit in the one place for too long. Your back will start playing up. Have you been stretching your legs regularly?'

'What?' she asked, caught off guard.

'Your legs. Have you been putting weight on them? One of the people I had lunch with happens to be a doctor and she told me that you should make sure not to shy away from exercising that ankle of yours or else when you do finally put weight on it, it'll be agony.'

'There was a doctor at the meeting?' was all she could find to say in response to this.

'No, don't be ridiculous, Mel. What would a doctor be doing at a business meeting between me and my chartered surveyor? I suppose it's conceivable that he might have been suffering from some bizarre illness that required twenty-four hour medical supervision, but then that wouldn't have been likely, would it? No, we met up with one or two people at lunch. Lizzie has a thriving practice in Maraval and her friends Gail and Monique do something or other in an advertising company. Interesting girls.'

'So interesting that you can't remember what they do exactly…' She grabbed the stack of typed letters and briskly tapped them against her thighs, straightening the papers, then she stared down at them with an efficient frown.

The black-printed words were a blur. She wasn't seeing them at all. In fact, she wasn't really seeing anything at all. She was too busy thinking, miserably, that for someone whose middle name had always been *Restraint,* her emotions appeared to have veered wildly out of control.

Lizzie? Gail? Monique? Probably three perfectly ordinary women, nothing much to look at, but she still felt racked with unreasonable jealousy at the thought of them talking to Robert, amusing him, capturing his imagination.

'The girls over here are quite something to look at, don't you think?' he mused, staring upwards at the ceiling and leaving her to the privacy of her raging thoughts. He shifted his eyes slyly across to her. 'And so *friendly,*' he murmured. 'Would you believe I've been invited to two parties already?'

'Good!' Melissa said brightly, focusing with glassy-eyed intensity on the indecipherable print in front of her. 'It's a brilliant idea to sample some of what the island has to offer.' She flicked through the letters, then did a bit more brisk tapping of them on her knees.

'Of course, you're invited, as well…'

'I'm not much of one for parties myself.' She looked up at him. 'I'm a dreadful bore as you well know.'

'I hate it when you put words into my mouth. Besides,' he

added airily, 'one of these parties happened to be tonight and I had to explain to them that I have my little invalid to look after.'

'I am *not* your invalid!' Melissa snapped. She slammed the letters down on the desk and folded her arms belligerently across her chest. 'I wouldn't *dream* of standing in your way of a good time, tonight or any other night for that matter. I'm *perfectly capable* of looking after myself and if you *dare* tell me once more about your responsibilities as my employer, I'll *throw* the heaviest object I can find straight at you!'

Tears of frustration and anger were gathering in the corners of her eyes and she blindly looked away, even though the computer terminal was now nothing but a blur.

With one surreptitious hand, she rubbed her eyes vigorously and tried to stifle the emergence of any giveaway sobbing, choking sounds.

'What's the matter? What's wrong?'

His urgent, concerned voice was close enough to her ear for her to draw back in horror. An unappealing snuffle threatened to surface and she sniffed it back, accepting the handkerchief that was thrust into her hands without looking at him.

'Tell me, Mel. What the hell is wrong? What's upset you?' He caressed the nape of her neck, under her sweep of dark hair, massaging and kneading it gently. His voice was thick and husky with worry, which only made her gulp and feel worse. She didn't want to be his responsibility or anyone else's for that matter.

'Nothing,' she muttered thickly, and he carefully tilted her chin until she was facing him, though her eyes remained stubbornly downcast.

'What did I say to upset you?' he whispered. He was still stroking her hair away from her face. 'If I wanted to go to some damned party, then I would, believe me. You know me well enough to know that I'm perfectly capable of going my own way if I want to, hang the rest of the world. Is that what's upset you? The fact that you think you're forcing me to be somewhere I would rather not be? Is that it? Tell me.'

'I've been a nuisance, with this ankle, hobbling around like an invalid. Hardly much of an asset, am I? Less than a week into my stint and I can't function!'

'You're feeling sorry for yourself, Mel…'

'And why not!' Her head shot up. 'Why shouldn't I?' She glared at him balefully. 'Who else do I have to feel sorry for me?'

May tomorrow never come, she thought as soon as the words were out of her mouth.

'Is it being here?' he asked quietly. 'Has this place brought back too many memories for you? Somehow I imagined that you might have relished returning to some old stamping ground.'

His voice was very soothing. Lulling even. Or maybe she was just going into some strange hypnotic trance induced by the mild breeze, the sound of the overhead fan, and too little food in her stomach.

'Why? If I had ever wanted to return to my *old stamping ground* as you put it, then I would have. I never returned here because I have quite a few unpleasant memories of it. You see,' she paused and her voice trembled when she spoke, 'this was where my mother's marriage to my stepfather all fell apart. The marriage fell apart and so, coincidentally, did my mother. In that order. Most of my years here were spent with their arguing voices ringing in my ears.

Leaving was a relief, even though the bitterness never ended for my mother. Oh, no, sir, she carried that all the way to her grave and she made sure that I was fully aware of every moment of her suffering. Men were all scoundrels and my stepfather had been the ringleader of them all. You would have thought that no one had ever experienced the same ordeal that she had. Although,' Melissa sighed wearily, 'I suppose putting up with all of that when you're not even in your own territory must have been terrifying. Such a small island. The whole world knew about what my stepfather was up to and with whom and by the time I hit eleven, so did I, courtesy of the other kids in the school.'

'That must have been horrendous,' he murmured in a low voice, and she closed her eyes, reliving the moment. 'I'm sorry I dragged you here. You can book the next flight out if you want and I'll see what I can do about rustling up a replacement out here.'

For the merest second of a heartbeat, she toyed with the idea of running back to England, away from the uncomfortable flux of emotions which had been stirred into life under the tropical sun. She knew that without him around, in these odd circumstances, her wildly out-of-sync heart would once again return to normal and when she did face him again, their relationship would have returned to its old familiar footing.

Temptation lasted no more than the length of time it took to blink your eye.

'Don't be silly,' she said, opening her eyes to look directly into his. 'I'm here to do a job and here is where I shall stay. If you can overlook the unsightly limping for the next day or two.' She gave him a shaky smile.

'Good girl.' A fraction too long. His eyes held hers for just a fraction too long. 'Because I do believe I couldn't do this thing without you…'

'What thing?' He stood up and she raised her face to look at him.

'This hotel thing…sorting out business thing…living thing…take your pick…'

There was the sound of rushing in her ears, which she quickly smothered. 'And I don't think I could do *this* thing without *you,*' she quipped lightly. 'You know…this *eating* thing. I haven't had a bite since breakfast so would you mind…?'

'It would be my deepest pleasure.'

CHAPTER SEVEN

'YOU'RE fussing.'

'I'm trying to make sure that you don't go hurtling down and crack your ankle again.'

'That was *three weeks ago!* I think it's safe to say that I'm steady on my feet now and am perfectly capable of manipulating a few rocks and uneven ground.'

'Don't forget that this was the site of the disaster.'

'I twisted my ankle! Hardly what I would call a *disaster!*' But she didn't pull her arm away. Over the past three weeks, which had seen her variously working like a slave and pampered like the invalid she certainly was not after the first few days, she had become accustomed to his casual touches. A helping hand here, an arm strategically placed there, the brush of his fingers as he placed a tray on her lap.

'Why are you being so solicitous?' she had asked suspiciously the first day he had insisted on bringing her a morning cup of tea in bed.

Robert Downe was brilliant, irascible, intolerant of stupidity, notoriously generous with his staff, sexy, witty, charming. Solicitous, he was not. Or at least not that Melissa had ever seen. In fact, he was the last man on the face of the earth she could ever imagine fretting around a woman. Women, his attitude had always indicated, were there to be wined and dined, courtesy of expensive restaurants. He freely admitted that entertaining them in his own space was something he preferred to steer clear from, just in case they *got ideas*.

'Because you can't move.'

'My ankle feels a bit stiff and my back's sore but I'm not *bedridden*.'

'No, but you might well be if you insist on taking things too quickly and leaping around the kitchen when you don't have to…'

Which had effectively shut her up because the thought of launching into a debate on whether she really intended to *leap around the kitchen* for the sake of a cup of tea, was enough to make her head spin.

And he had not stopped with the first cup of tea. He insisted that she put her feet up every three seconds and, bewilderingly, insisted on cooking the food for them both himself, even though Denise was more than happy to oblige.

He was, much to her amusement, an enthusiastic, adventurous and absolutely useless chef.

As soon as she regained her freedom of movement, she began to edit some of his creations, watching from a stool in the kitchen and tactfully restraining some of his more inappropriate combinations.

'I'm amazed,' Melissa said, looking around the plot of land, which was now furiously being worked on by a small army of labourers. She had not ventured out to see the plot of land since the accident and progress was being made in leaps and bounds.

'By the time we leave, the shell should more or less be finished, barring unforeseeable delays.' He was standing just behind her and she could feel the steady rise and fall of his chest as he inhaled and exhaled. The past few weeks in the sun had turned him a deep brown, just as it had turned her a similar colour. Conversely her hair seemed to have become a shade lighter. Now, the ends of her two stumpy plaits were burnished gold.

'Look over there.' He casually curled his long fingers along her soft upper arm and pointed to a completed section of the hotel. 'You can see what the eventual layout of the rooms will be like. Each room overlooking the sea. Huge windows so that the sea breeze can blow through.' His voice throbbed with enthusiasm, and she found herself smiling. 'Mosquito nets. I've always found mosquito nets disproportionately romantic.'

'So have I,' Melissa echoed softly, her eyes dreamily conjuring up the image he was painting. 'I would love to…' She stopped and flushed.

'…make love under one?' he finished for her.

'I didn't say that,' she replied promptly.

His voice was soothing, as though he was kindly trying to calm a ruffled child. 'No, of course you didn't. Now, shall I take you somewhere for lunch after I've had a quick word with the contractor? You've been stuck indoors for too long.'

'I've enjoyed it, actually. And I haven't been *stuck indoors*. I go for a swim every day around lunch-time and I do all my reviewing outside in the sun.'

'You didn't tell me you've been bathing in the sea.'

'I'm sure I mentioned it to you.'

'You didn't.'

'Well, I guess it didn't seem very important.' With day drawing to a close, the sun was far less fierce than it had been earlier on. The sound of the surf, as usual, was a steady pounding and her mind began to drift away down the road of mosquito nets and romantic evenings spent under them.

Her thoughts had never been as sensual as they were out here. Whilst before she might have contemplated the usefulness of a mosquito net, now she found herself deliberating on how much fun could be had under one. With the right person.

'Of course it's important!'

His explosion surprised her enough into looking up at him, squinting against the dull glare, and not quite sure whether she had confused the ferocity of his response with the sound of building work.

'What if something happened to you? That beach is deserted! For God's sake, woman, don't you use your head!'

Melissa stiffened. 'I'm a strong swimmer, Robert. And more to the point, I'm not a child. There's no need for you to supervise me!'

'There is if you indulge in such recklessness as bathing there when there's no one else around to help if you happen to get into trouble. And what about your injuries?' he demanded, as an afterthought. 'What about your back and your ankle? You might be able to swim across the channel in optimum conditions but even you would have to admit that you'd be a fool to risk your life swimming when you're disabled.'

Melissa's mouth dropped open at the thunderous expression on his face.

Was the man deranged? Had the heat scrambled his brains? And if not, couldn't he see how insulting it was to be accused of crass stupidity? Was he quaking at the thought of what obscure rules she had been contravening in the wretched Employer/Employee code book by actually doing something off her own bat, without him around to say yea or nay?

'I didn't realise that I had to ask your permission before I drew breath,' she said coolly, and he groaned in frustration and ran his fingers through his hair, which was longer now in the absence of any nearby hairdresser to keep it regularly cropped short.

'That's not what I'm saying.'

'Well, it certainly sounds that way to me.' She walked off towards the edge of the land and looked down at the rolling sea beneath. The incline down to it was gentle, a bank of bush and trees that swayed in the breeze, a mass of sharp greens and yellows and browns that formed a continuous carpet until the fine grainy sand took over.

She felt him next to her but didn't look around.

She was fiercely independent. So, she imagined, was he. So why then was it that he couldn't see how loathsome it was for her to feel like a supplicant, someone in need of someone else's shoulder to lean on. The fact that she had actually *enjoyed* leaning on him, even when she really no longer needed to, was something she uneasily chose to overlook.

'I think I'll head back now,' she said, addressing the panoramic view in front of her and ignoring the rather more menacing one next to her.

'Why?' he demanded bluntly. 'There are still some things I want to point out to you so that we can tally it all with the drawings later.'

Melissa looked at him and sighed. She knew she had no choice but that any such prolonged tour was hardly necessary.

'Fine.'

'The pool will be over there. We had to alter the original plan to accommodate *that* crop of coconut trees that I wanted left untouched. I was concerned about you. All right? There was no need to react as though I'd maliciously committed a crime.' His profile was hard and unyielding and stubborn. With a sudden burst of clarity, she glimpsed the boy of ten, a miniature version of the man standing mutinously next to her, his arm almost but not quite touching hers. A young, dark-haired, reckless daredevil who would dig his heels in should anyone try and stand in his way. Lord, but he must have been a handful! She almost smiled at the thought of it.

'Thank you for your concern,' she compromised in a polite voice and he turned to glare at her.

'Politeness is the most effective way of squashing someone else's foul mood, but it won't work, Mel. You act as though I'd insulted you by voicing my concern and I want to know why.'

'And *I* want to know why you're getting so hot under the collar about something as trivial as my taking a dip in the sea when you're not around. I paddle, Robert! My feet never stop touching the bottom! I know how unpredictable the water here can be!' She began walking away and he fell into step with her. 'Women,' she said, flashing him a sidelong, withering look, 'no longer need to consult a man every time they want to do something. In case you haven't noticed, we now make informed choices and use our own heads in the process!'

'How could I fail to notice?' he fired back, 'you've been working for me for the past three years, haven't you?'

'Is there an implied insult there somewhere?' Melissa stopped, put her hands on her hips and looked at him narrowly.

'Not that I'm aware of, although since I clearly have no idea what goes on in women's heads, I'm probably wrong.'

Storm waves were gathering in Melissa's head and what made matters worse was the fact that she knew full well *why.* If nothing else the past three weeks were a lesson in how susceptible the average person is to someone else's attention. She had always stood on her own two feet, even as a young girl. Her mother's muttered complaints, instead of eroding her self-confidence, had forged a kind of closed resilience in her that had gradually, over the years, turned into an inability to open up to other people. Any vulnerabilities had always been neatly hidden under her hard-working efficiency. She had worked hard at school, hard at college, hard at work and if men had been turned off by that, then she had never really thought about it.

Robert, intensely masculine as he was, had managed to worm his way under her skin with his sudden gentle consideration for her. The fact that he had succeeded in convincing her that he was enjoying every minute of his new-fangled personality had only made him more appealing. Now it hurt to admit that she had confused his easy compliance with his inborn sense of responsibility towards an employee.

'Yes,' she snapped, worked up, 'you probably are.' She headed forcefully in the direction of the house, arms folded across her chest, chin jutting out, and when he continued to meet her pace, she said, without looking at him, 'I thought you wanted to have a word with your contractor. *Please* don't let me stand in your way.'

'I wouldn't dream of letting you stand in my way. After all, we men *do* occasionally make informed choices, as well, you know. I can call Bob in the morning.'

Her skin was prickling with anger by the time they arrived back at the house and she could feel her whole body rigid and tightly strung like a piece of elastic pulled to its full stretching point. If she so much as looked at him, she would probably snap and snapping was out of the question. Raging, hurt, insulted and mortified by the ferocity of her own response she might well be. She was also still his secretary and secretaries, however well they worked with their bosses, were not indispensable.

If she didn't control her wayward temper, she might well find herself out of a job and the thought of leaving Robert, never seeing him again…

She pushed a trembling hand through her hair and feverishly contemplated what her brain had obligingly locked away for longer than she cared to think. She could feel the perspiration glistening on her skin like droplets of water and her body was engulfed in a fierce, burning heat as she blindly made her way to the kitchen and poured herself something to drink.

'Look. I apologise for…well, for losing it back there,' Melissa said, speaking to but not looking in the direction of the man glowering by the entrance to the kitchen. She took a long, shaky breath and a deep gulp of cold juice. 'I guess the heat got to me.' So this was what Love felt like. Wonderful, marvellous Love that put foolish grins on people's faces and made them think that they could do anything. She never anticipated that it could also make you feel as though a knife was being turned very slowly somewhere deep in your gut. She had always imagined that that sort of thing happened when everything had turned sour.

'Losing it is nothing to be ashamed of. We all do it from time to time.'

'Perhaps you're right.' She finished the juice, made a production out of washing, and then when she had no option but to turn around and face him, she said, eyes still lowered, 'I think I'll go and have a shower now.'

He stepped aside to let her pass and she knew that the hairs on her arm were standing on end as she brushed past him. She *knew* now, knew that her forbidden love for him had inalterably changed everything between them. She would never be able to look at him again, hear his voice, watch the way he moved, without desire clawing through her body like burning iron spikes, ripping her to shreds. A few seconds of revelation had destroyed everything.

Her mind was churning as she stepped under the shower, turning it to *cold* in a vain attempt to wash away her gut-wrenching panic.

A little under three weeks left to go. She would have to endure it the best she could, but the minute she returned to England, she would hand in her notice.

She dried, then peered into the huge bathroom mirror to see if she could glimpse any noticeable changes in her face. A woman in love should *glow,* shouldn't she? Even if love had wreaked havoc with her sanity? There was, she noted sadly, no glow. Her skin was flushed, true enough, but there was nothing radiant about the woman staring back at her.

She had a small hand towel wrapped turban style around her hair and the bath towel barely skimming her body when she pushed open the bathroom door into the bedroom.

There he was, leaning against the door, hands thrust into

his pockets, casually relaxed. The air-conditioning, which she had turned on as soon as she entered the bedroom, to combat the raging heat coursing through her, had obviously drowned out the sound of the door opening and closing.

'What are you doing here!' Melissa said, when her vocal cords had finally caught up with her brain. She clutched the towel tightly at the top and at the same time lowered the other hand to the bottom of the thigh-skirting piece of cloth.

'I came to finish our conversation.'

'Well you can get out because my bedroom is no place for continuing a conversation! And you should have knocked!'

'I did,' he protested meekly, 'but no one answered and I just came in when I found it was unlocked.'

Melissa's feet appeared to be tacked to the floor with invisible nails, as did the hand gripping the towel for dear life.

'It's time we sorted this thing out once and for all.' He pushed himself away from the door and strolled lazily towards her while she, unable to flee, struggled with a sickening sense of mounting panic.

'Sorted *what* out?' she squeaked, her heart gathering momentum the closer he got.

'Us. What's been happening between us.'

He was dangerously close to her now, looking down at the faint shadow of cleavage visible above the tautly pulled towel.

'I don't know what you're talking about,' Melissa babbled hysterically. 'One minute you're accusing me of being a lunatic for having the occasional dip in the sea when you're not around, the next minute you're ranting on about *us.* I'm your secretary! You're my boss! I thought we understood one another!' She could feel herself almost on the verge of tears at his bewildering intrusion into her bedroom and cuttingly pertinent choice of conversation, given what she had spent the past hour brooding over.

'We do understand one another. Therein lies the problem.'

He raised his hands to her shoulders and began rotating the pads of his thumbs against the sides of her neck. Melissa emitted a strangled sound and fought a desperate need to sink to the floor, rag doll style. 'I always knew we worked well together, but it's only since coming here that I've realised how much further it goes between us.' His voice was low and smoky and sent shivers racing up and down her spine. 'And don't try to pretend that you haven't felt it, too.'

He had inclined his body forward so that his lips brushed her hair and his voice was barely audible. 'You've enjoyed all those accidental touches, as much as I've enjoyed doing it, feeling the charge running between us like an unstoppable electric current.' He blew into her ear and then his tongue flicked against her earlobe, squirmed into the delicate dip just above. Melissa moaned softly and bravely but ineffectively flattened her palms against his chest and attempted to push him away.

Instead of responding to the half-hearted pressure, he covered her hands with his, then raised them, one at a time, to his mouth so that he could flutter kisses on the tender flesh of her inner wrist.

'I've been wanting to do this for weeks,' he breathed shakily. 'In fact, I suspect that I may have wanted to do this for far longer than that.' One finger slipped a centimetre under the top of the towel. A few centimetres lower, Melissa's nipples pulsed into life, pushing against the rough cotton of the towel.

'No.' Was that a protest? To her own ears, it sounded like a feeble avowal of defeat!

He laughed softly under his breath. 'Why am I unconvinced by that?' His mouth found the slender column of her neck and she arched back to accommodate his nuzzling exploration of it, sinking back and feeling sweet relief when he picked her up and carried her to the bed.

'No, don't,' he rasped, when she moved to pull aside the

towel which for some reason she was still clutching in a rigor mortis grip. 'Let me. I want to savour every glorious moment of this. I've waited long enough.'

Her mind snagged on the *every glorious moment,* and she smiled a radiant, feline smile of pure satisfaction, moving sinuously against the sheets, her eyes half closed, her damp, unbrushed hair framing the small, smooth face so that she looked like a wild child.

He uttered a sound that was halfway between triumph and craving and knelt between her legs so that he could better see as he yanked down the towel, exposing her small, pointed breasts and the patch of soft, downy hair between her thighs. Thighs which she opened to accommodate his greedy, needy gaze, pleasure and passion filling her as his eyes darkened with hunger.

When he touched her, she could feel the burning urgency in him which he was trying to control, and the knowledge of that gave her a heady sense of power. She closed her eyes, every pore in her body attuned to the man towering over her. When she knew that he was stripping off his clothes, she felt a quiver of nerves, but kept her eyes firmly closed until he resumed his position between her legs, then she opened her eyes and feasted on the throbbing, jutting manhood that proclaimed his desire more fiercely than any words could.

With a purring smile, she raised her hands above her head, inviting him to touch her wherever he wanted and sizzling as his mouth clasped over one nipple and he began sucking at it, drawing it into the wetness of his mouth, while his fingers played with her other nipple, provoking the tight, brown bud into glorious arousal. As she squirmed against the sheets, her legs opening, the cool air from the air-conditioner caressed the inside of her thighs. She raised her legs so that her slender feet brushed erotically against his erection and with a groan he moved down to capture the honeyed moisture of her aroused with his tongue.

By the time she felt flashpoint nearing, his tongue had already invaded her most private parts. The throbbing bud had swollen but before she could quiver to orgasm, he raised himself and thrust into her, rhythmically and forcefully, over and over and over, a complete masculine possession that sent her senses spinning into orbit and filled her with the deepest, sweetest feeling that at last, things all made sense.

CHAPTER EIGHT

FROM behind the bedroom window, Melissa stood and surveyed the neat parameters of her garden with very little satisfaction. Summer should, by now, have been disposing of what had been a very lukewarm Spring. Instead, the days fluctuated between the promise of warmth and the spiteful deliverance of yet more rain. The coolest June, it was repeated on the weather reports every so often, since records began.

Behind her, her tan suitcase was packed although now that the taxi to the airport was imminent, she was torn by the certainty that the holiday which she had booked in a moment of maudlin self-pity, had been a very bad idea.

The past can never be revisited, she thought, staring out beyond the rectangle of the garden to the road. Melissa wished that she had had the wit to realise it a little earlier, like when she had found herself in the travel agency, scouting through brochures for warm holidays, pausing as a certain familiar sight accosted her eyes for a hotel, newly opened, in the divine solitude of the sea and forests of Trinidad. He must have paid the earth to have it included in the exclusive brochure at the last possible moment and just in time for the summer trippers.

She had stared at the picture, hands trembling, and thought, *So this is how it all turned out in the end.* Even more spectacular than her wildest imaginings. She remembered in those heady remaining weeks, when they had worked and played with abandon, that they had chosen the colour for the outside facade. A startling blue, the same colour as the sea, with white fretwork and wrought iron providing eye-catching contrast. Seeing it reproduced in the exclusive *Elegant Caribbean* brochure, glossy and enticing, had sent her shocked heart into immediate overdrive. It had also sent her mourning soul into wild temporary insanity that had seen her booking a week's vacation on the spot, using a different name for the hotel booking, *just in case.*

She heard the sound of the doorbell and when she focused her eyes on the road, she realised that the taxi had arrived. Her mind had taken flight and winged its way back into the past, as though it hadn't had enough of it over the past two and a half months. How much more was it possible to dwell on a past without collapsing from an overdose?

She grabbed the case, which was small and pleasantly light, and as she locked the front door, the full force of her stupidity hit her like a bucket of cold water.

Why was she going to the hotel for a holiday? What exactly was the point of *that?* She had spent the past three weeks convincing herself that the only way she would ever be able to deal with Robert was to revisit the spot that had been the site of all the cataclysmic changes that had happened to her, put the whole episode to rest, so to speak.

Now, in a flash, she realised that going back was only going to further her misery. She wouldn't *put thoughts of Robert to rest,* she would revive them, not that they needed much reviving anyway. She would spend an entire week wallowing in self-pity and grief. She would, she was now convinced, as the taxi trundled off to the airport, be surrounded by an invisible aura of unspeakable, harrowing depression that would probably frighten off the other guests. After all, what could be more off-putting for her fellow holiday-makers, out for a jolly, relaxing vacation, than the sight of a miserable, heart-broken woman sitting alone in a corner of the lounge glugging back rum and Cokes and trying to stave off a nervous collapse?

She rested her chin in the palm of her hand and peered out of the car window.

Whichever way she went, it all came back to Robert.

She wished to God that she could forget, but the minute she opened her eyes in the morning, she was instantly besieged by memories.

The sex, she knew, she would never forget and would never want to. Every minute, replayed in her mind, was to be savoured, as was the memory of how complete and fulfilled she had felt when his lips had touched her and she had felt herself blossom under his caresses.

Hard on the heels of those thoughts, however, were a host of others. Just conjuring up an image of him was like opening a Pandora's box.

She closed her eyes and recalled the plane flight back, when she had sunk into herself, already reerecting the defences she had willingly allowed him to demolish. He had slept through most of the trip back, which had been a blessing, and when he *had* tried to talk to her, she had clammed up and feigned exhaustion. After all, it *had* been a night flight and she *had* been tired.

When they hit England, everything happened so quickly that it had been possible, just, to ignore the increasingly impatient look smouldering in the depths of his eyes. When he had held her arm and demanded an explanation for her weird behaviour, she had taken refuge behind an apologetic smile and some mumbled excuse about a headache from the pressurised cabin of the plane.

'I just need to think about...what happened between us...' she had pleaded softly. 'Please, *please,* try and understand…could we talk about this next week? Give me the weekend to recover…'

He hadn't liked it, but he had grudgingly agreed. With his typical, forthright aggression, he had seen her delaying tactics as cowardly, but he hadn't pressed her and for that she had been grateful.

She doubted whether he would have been as accommodating if he had seen the thoughts scrambling through her head.

Forty-eight hours after they had said an awkward goodbye to one another at the terminal, he would have been all too aware of every thought. Every thought but the big, important one, because the word *Love* had been nowhere in the resignation letter waiting to greet him on the Monday morning.

It had been carefully constructed. It spoke coolly of the impossibility of ever working together, it contained enough thank-yous to strip it of any personal emotion whatsoever, and most importantly it implored that he accept the situation along with her most profound regrets and make no attempt to confront her face to face.

We were a little incautious and perhaps what happened might serve as a reminder of where lust can get someone, but I hope you will remember me on friendly terms as I shall remember you.

As an exercise in detachment, the letter had been beautifully worded. She had crept like a thief into the office on the Sunday, deposited it on his desk, had a final look around, cleared her few personal possessions from her desk, and left the way she had come, depositing her office key with a bemused Frank at the reception desk.

Her only consolation was that she was sparing herself further hurt by leaving as she did. Robert Downe didn't love her and not once had the word passed his lips. *Want* had been a frequent intruder in his vocabulary, but *wanting* and *loving* were world's apart and without the one, the other was, in the long term, unacceptable. At least to her.

She knew that he had wanted their affair to continue. He had assumed that she would have no problem with that. The fact that it would, by nature of its foundation, be temporary, was something he appeared not to have considered.

When your heart's not involved the termination of a relationship becomes a formality, she had reasoned over the past two months, a hiccup that you can put behind you with no effort at all. She would be the only loser.

'Going anywhere nice?' the taxi-driver asked, eyeing her in the rear-view mirror.

'Nope. It's going to be a horrendous week and if I hadn't paid for the thing, I wouldn't be going at all.' That had silenced him, and she had slumped back into her repetitive, unwelcome line of thought.

It proved so tiring that she ended up sleeping a good deal of the flight away, only rousing herself when the captain announced that they were about to land in Barbados. Thirty-five minutes to go and they would be in Trinidad. As she blinked herself wide awake, she could anticipate her oncoming nightmare with depressing clarity.

By the time the plane landed and she found herself sitting in the back of one of the few taxis available for hire at the airport, she had resigned herself to her situation with a certain amount of fateful calm. The prospect of one week of unrelieved depression was beginning to feel masochistically satisfying, especially if she could convince her usually alcohol-free body to immerse itself in seven nights of splendid, helpful inebriation.

Unfortunately, by the time the long, winding drive was completed, and she had paid the taxi-driver, it was too dark to make out much of the outside of the hotel. The lights interspersed around the wide veranda circling the hotel were only able to give a tantalising glimpse of blue and white. Tables and chairs were informally dotted on the wooden deck and guests were milling around in shorts and T-shirts, drinking and chatting. There was something inescapably old-fashioned and sedate about the whole scene and Melissa thought that if Robert were here, he would be thrilled to see his completed work and its residents.

Inside was small but exquisite. She was efficiently welcomed by a beaming woman in her forties with impossibly white teeth and impossibly smooth skin and her bag was whisked away with such speed that she only had a brief glimpse of the decor before being shown to her room.

It felt strange and unsettling to be looking at the fruition of what had started out as a dream on a piece of paper.

Her mind seemed to stop totally at Memory platform and her eyes were blurring over with unshed tears by the time she hustled the porter out of the spacious, wooden-floored room. She would have her breakfast in her room in the morning. She *had* to. The thought of chatting politely with the other guests and skimming over the fact that she was intimately connected with the hotel was something she would have to work up to.

With the anticipation of a sleepless night, she was surprised, on hearing a gentle knock on her bedroom door, that she had slept like a log. It was eight-thirty and when she staggered drowsily out of bed and pulled back the curtains, it was to find the sun shining in all its glory.

'Breakfast, Miss James,' a local voice said, and she stuck on her dressing gown and gazed out of the window as the bustle of trays was heard behind her. When she heard the bedroom door click shut, she turned around.

The sight of Robert leaning against the wall by the door was shocking enough to make her rub her eyes. For a mirage, he looked remarkably real!

'Surprise, surprise.'

Mirages didn't hold conversations. Her legs felt weak and she half stumbled into the soft, comfy chair next to her.

'Breakfast?' He lifted the silver lid covering the plate, one hand still in his trouser pocket. 'Your favourite. Coconut bread, scrambled eggs, some cheese. Aren't you suitably flattered at the personal service?' He flashed her a hard, cynical smile while she continued to stare at him with her mouth half open, goldfish style. A goldfish that has suddenly found its bowl invaded by a piranha.

'Maybe not,' he mused, replacing the lid and strolling towards her, stopping en route to look through the window at the meltingly beautiful vista stretching down below. 'Why should you be?' He perched on the window ledge and gave her a long, withering look to which she could find no suitable response save for some more inelegant opening and closing of her mouth. Shock was still in total command of her vocal cords. 'You obviously weren't impressed by anything else about me judging from the way you vanished in a puff of smoke with no warning at all.' His jaw tightened and she watched, fascinated, at the rapid beating of the pulse in his throat.

'I can explain,' she croaked, a little wildly. Why he had taken this long to demand an explanation, she couldn't understand but next to her electrifying shock was a fierce, illicit thrill of setting eyes on him again, even under these circumstances. 'I thought…you do remember that I said…that I mentioned…I needed to think…I thought th-that it would be easier all…'

'Do you know how I felt when I found that miserable, unrevealing excuse of a note?' he bellowed, his dark eyebrows meeting in a thunderous frown.

Melissa gulped. *And how do you think I felt when I discovered that I'd fallen in love with you? Chipper? Overjoyed? Ready to rush out and start buying bed linen for our shared life together?* 'I would have told you…face to face…but…'

'You liar!' He advanced towards her and she pushed herself back into the chair.

'Why now?' she whispered, as he towered over her cringing form. 'Why have you decided to...were you here all along? Did you spot me when I arrived and thought that you might as well have it out...?'

He leaned over her, breathing heat from every pore, his arms like steel rods on either side. 'I couldn't believe what I was reading when I got that note. I had to reread the damn thing over and over. Look at it!' He took a crumpled piece of paper out of his pocket and flung it on her lap. 'Read it! Go on! Go on!'

She falteringly read the first line and a half and then dried up.

'I wanted to come after you,' he grated harshly. 'God knows, I wanted to break down your damn door and throttle you until I got a sensible answer out of you! Weeks in each other's company and...' He raked his fingers through his hair. 'But no way. *No way* was I going to hound you down. As far as I was concerned, you could take a running leap. The sea is full of fish. Positively *brimming over* with them!'

'So I'm sure you've snapped up one or two already!' Melissa was stung into replying. His face darkened as he lowered brooding, blue eyes for a few seconds before raising them to hers accusingly.

'As a matter of fact I haven't,' he threw at her. He walked towards the window and stared out while Melissa watched him compulsively.

'Why didn't you come and find me before?' she asked his profile. The disappointed accusatory tone of her voice left a sour taste in her mouth, but she knew that his lack of pursuit had hurt far, far more than she had expected. For the first week after she had left her job, she had daily expected him to show up on her doorstep, a hulking, angry figure of rejected male, if only to lambaste her with his contempt for her behaviour.

In her head, she rehearsed a number of approaches she could take to his appearance on her doorstep.

As the days lengthened into weeks, she gradually and bitterly accepted that her absence in his life had simply not meant enough for him to pursue her. He didn't' want to show her his anger, he didn't even want to ask her what the hell she thought she was up to, walking out of her job and leaving him in the lurch when she was required by law to work a month's notice. She had pitifully clung to the belief that he *must* get in touch, if only to ask some boring, technical question to do with work, but time had killed any such expectation.

'Give me one good reason why I should have.'

'Okay. Why have you sought me out *now?*'

He turned to face her fully, his face dark and glowering. 'Because…' he began. A look of hesitation darkened his face and he flushed uncomfortably.

'I don't think you were here already and spotted me arriving,' Melissa said to herself. 'When the booking was made, I specifically asked my travel agent to make sure that you weren't around. I told her that you owned the place but I wanted to be here when you weren't because we had been through a bad patch and I couldn't face you…'

'Why couldn't you face me?' he asked quickly, and she looked at him distractedly.

'Let me finish. *How* did you know that I'd be here? Did you book your trip at the last minute? Is it just coincidence that we're both here at the same time?' She had no idea what to make of the surreal situation. She knew that she should be enraged at his sudden appearance in her life just when she had accepted that she would never see him again, but all she felt was a soaring joy and satisfaction at seeing his face, a frustrating, infuriating reaction that made a nonsense of all the common sense mini lectures she had delivered to herself on a daily basis for the past few weeks.

'You can't blame a man...' he muttered, folding his arms and glaring at her perplexed frown. 'Most men would have done exactly what I did...'

'What are you talking about?'

'I decided that I wasn't going to chase you down...I've never run behind any woman in my life before...' He raked his fingers through his hair and shook his head in frustration. He frowned and stared at the wall behind her. 'If you couldn't incorporate what we had going into life over here, then that was *your* choice. It wasn't my business to try and talk you out of it.'

'So why are you here?' Melissa repeated.

'Because none of it worked. I've spent every day thinking...about you...it's driving me to distraction. A week after you left...I...employed a private detective to follow you...'

'You what!'

'You heard me!' he rasped defensively, moving towards her. 'You were driving me crazy!'

'So now it's all my fault, is it?' She tried to feel insulted but a soft smile curved her lips and he fell to his knees to stare into her face. He picked up one of her small, slender hands and turned it over and over in his big palm.

'I was too proud,' he muttered. 'I knew that I'd fallen in love with you but I couldn't stand the thought of rejection and I was too proud to follow you and ask you what you felt, what I had meant to you...'

Fallen in love, fallen in love, fallen in love... When? Shouldn't she have been able to spot a man in love? She peered into his face to see whether he was joking, and when he returned her stare levelly, she whispered, in a numb voice, 'You mean it, don't you?'

'Every word. I fell in love with you. While I was going along my merry way, working hard and playing hard, I fell in love with you and I think, at the back of my mind, that's part of the reason why I went to Trinidad to put up the hotel.

Some part of me wanted you so badly that I just wanted to *be* in the place where you'd grown up. I thought that I could somehow find the key to your soul if only I knew more about your past. You were so damned cagey! I wanted you to open up to me, long before we ended up on the island, and I was prepared to travel halfway across the world to try and unlock the door.

'If you're not ready for all this…I'm prepared to wait, but when I found out where you were heading, I knew that I had to get over here and finally have this all out. I couldn't live with the pain of being apart from you for a second longer.'

'Are you sure,' Melissa said gravely, while her spirit took flight and discovered Heaven, 'that all this has nothing to do with the fact that you can't find a replacement secretary?' She smiled slowly at him, her eyes brimming with the love she had dared not speak before and he returned her smile with a blissful one of his own.

'Which reminds me,' he said, kissing each of her fingers, 'there are a couple of things I can't find…'

'You should have called me earlier…'

'You should never have left me,' he returned with a sulky, little-boy grin. 'Fortunately, I have a solution for that…'

'Which is?' As if she couldn't guess!

'You'll just have to marry me, my darling Miss James…' He pulled one of her fingers into his mouth and sucked it until the sigh that came from her lips and the adjusting of her position had less to do with discomfort and more to do with her body wanting him to suck rather a lot more than one finger.

'Before I find speaking impossible,' Melissa gasped, as he pulled aside her bathrobe and delicately licked the raised, tight bud of her nipple, 'I'd better agree.' She ran her fingers through his hair and sighed with deep happiness, 'I love you, Robert Downe. I can't remember a time when…I didn't.'

And then she slipped forward in the chair, pulling apart her bathrobe entirely and succumbing to the sweetness of his mouth caressing every minute pore of her yearning body.

She would have this…today, tomorrow and forever….

EPILOGUE

'IT LOOKS different. Does it look different to you?' Melissa looked at the walls, the decor, the abundance of plants that seemed to be waiting patiently in their plant pots before staging a complete takeover of the foyer. She couldn't put her finger on *what* was different, but she knew that something was.

'It looks lived in,' the tall, dark man standing next to her said. 'Not so new and shiny.'

'A bit like you, in other words,' she said with a grin, and he bent to kiss the corner of her mouth, as though unable to resist the fleeting touch.

'What do you expect?' Robert asked, sighing elaborately, his hand pressed into the curve of her back, a strong, warm, deeply satisfying pressure that would never, she knew, lose its ability to thrill her.

Melissa didn't have to turn her head for the expression in his voice to bring a contented smile to her face.

'I do nothing but work!'

'You poor baby.' Melissa oozed amused sympathy.

'Pleasing three women isn't an easy task, even for someone like me, a man in his prime, at the peak of his physical prowess...and two of them don't even seem to appreciate my efforts!' In unison they glanced at the little figures lying in the double buggy in front of them. Identical girls, a little over six months and already, as he was fond of saying, particularly when holding them both close to his chest, showing every indication of being as stubborn and demanding as their mother.

'Oh, they do.' Melissa tousled the thatch of black hair that sprang with identical lushness from the tiny, exquisite faces. In reply, there was a whimper which never made it to a cry because Robert scooped up the grumbling infant, holding her out in front of him and inspecting her with the pride of a man utterly in love with the product of his virility. Bright blue eyes stared back at him and the lower lip wobbled, threatening to cry.

'This is your hotel,' he murmured, 'and your sister's...and you'll be coming here every year, at least once a year because your mother tells me that she prefers the weather over here to the weather in England.'

'That's not what *I* tell them,' Melissa said, with a gurgle of amusement, savouring this moment of shared intimacy in the darkness of the outside veranda, before they were spied by the zealous Vanessa at reception and ushered in with pomp and ceremony.

'And what, might I ask, *do* you tell them, Mrs. Downe?'

'Why, that their father's a sentimental dear, of course! Which is one of the reasons why I adore him... So much masculine virility concealing such a big, soft heart!'

'Keep your voice down, woman! Walls have ears, you know!' He paused and then tickled her ear with his tongue and whispered, 'But you're right about the masculine, virile part. Tonight, my darling, I'll show you just how masculine and just how virile your adoring husband is...'

Melissa chuckled and looked at him, meeting his eyes with tenderness, 'And the girls...?'

'Are under instructions not to disturb...' He sighed. 'I hope!'